Also by Andrew Clements

*The Landry News*

*Frindle*

# Andrew Clements

**ALADDIN PAPERBACKS**

New York   London   Toronto   Sydney   Singapore

First Aladdin Paperbacks edition September 2001
Copyright © 2000 by Andrew Clements
Aladdin Paperbacks
An imprint of Simon & Schuster
Children's Publishing Division
1230 Avenue of the Americas
New York, NY 10020

Also available in a Simon & Schuster Books for Young Readers hardcover edition.

Designed by Steve Scott
The text for this book was set in Garth Graphic.
Manufactured in the United States of America
16 18 20 19 17 15

The Library of Congress has cataloged the hardcover edition as follows:
Clements, Andrew, 1949-
The janitor's boy / Andrew Clements.—1st ed.
p.   cm.
Summary: Fifth grader Jack finds himself the target of ridicule at school when
it becomes known that his father is one of the janitors,
and he turns his anger onto his father.
ISBN-13: 978-0-689-81818-9 (hc.)
ISBN-10: 0-689-81818-1 (hc.)
[1. Janitors—Fiction.  2. Fathers and sons—Fiction.  3. Schools—Fiction.]
I. Title
PZ7.C59118 Jan  2000
[Fic]—dc21
99-047457
ISBN-13: 978-0-689-83585-8 (Aladdin pbk.)
ISBN-10: 0-689-83585-X (Aladdin pbk.)

## Chapter 1

# The Perfect Crime

Jack Rankin had a particularly sensitive nose. As he walked into school in the morning, sometimes he would pause in the entryway and pull in a snoot-load of air from the flow rushing out the door. Instantly he could tell what the cafeteria lunch would be, right down to whether the Jell-O was strawberry or orange. He could tell if the school secretary was wearing perfume, and whether there was an open box of doughnuts on the table in the teachers room on the second floor.

On this particular Monday morning Jack's nose was on high alert. He was working on a special project—a bubble gum project. Today's activity was the result of about a week's worth of research and planning.

Days ago, Jack had begun the project by secretly examining the bottoms of desks and tables all over the school, trying to decide exactly which kind of discarded gum was the most unpleasant.

After he conducted his first few sniff tests, he didn't even have to look underneath a table or a chair to tell if there was gum. The scent of the stuff followed him from class to class. He had gum on the brain. He smelled gum everywhere—on the bus, in the halls, passing a locker, walking into a classroom.

Jack finally chose watermelon Bubblicious. It had to be the smelliest gum in the universe. Even weeks after being stuck under a chair or table, that sickly sweet smell and distinctive crimson color were unmistakable. And Bubblicious, any flavor of it, was definitely the stickiest gum available. By Jack's calculations, it was more than three times stickier than Bazooka.

The final stage of Jack's gum caper began in today's third-period gym class. Mr. Sargent had them outside in the cool October air, running wind sprints to prepare for a timed mile next week. By the end of the period Jack had four pieces of gum in his mouth, chewed to maximum stickiness. The smell of it almost overpowered him.

Carefully steering a wide path around Mr. Sargent, he went to his locker before the next class. He spat the chewed gum into a sandwich bag he had brought from home. The bag had two or three tablespoons of water in it to keep the gum from sticking to the plastic.

Jack sealed the bag, stuffed it into his pocket, and immediately jammed another two pieces of gum into his mouth and started to chew.

He processed those two pieces plus two more during science, managed to chew up another four pieces during lunch period, and even finished one piece during math—quite an accomplishment in Mrs. Lambert's classroom.

By the time he got to music, he had thirteen chewed pieces of gum in a plastic bag in the pocket of his jeans—all warm and soft and sticky.

Monday-afternoon music class was the ideal crime scene. The room had four levels, stair-stepping down toward the front. The seats were never assigned, and Mr. Pike always made kids fill the class from the front of the room backward. By walking in the door just as the echo of the bell was fading, Jack was guaranteed a seat in the back row. He sat directly behind Jed Ellis, also known as Giant Jed. With no effort at all he was completely hidden from Mr. Pike.

The only other person in the back row was Kerry Loomis, sitting six seats away. She was hiding too, hunched over a notebook, trying to finish some homework. Jack had half a crush on Kerry. On a

3

normal day he would have tried to get her attention, make her laugh, show off a little. But today was anything but normal.

Mr. Pike was at the front of the room. Standing behind the upright piano, he pounded out a melody with one hand and flailed the air with his other one, trying to get fidgety fifth graders to sing their hearts out.

Jack Rankin was supposed to be singing along with the rest of the chorus. He was supposed to be learning a new song for the fall concert. The song was something about eagles soaring and being free and happy—not how Jack was feeling at this moment.

Bending down, Jack brought the baggie up to his mouth and stuffed in all thirteen pieces of gum for a last softening chew. The lump was bigger than a golf ball, and he nearly gagged as he worked it into final readiness, keeping one eye on the clock.

With one minute of class left, Mr. Pike was singing along now, his head bobbing like a madman, urging the kids to open their mouths wider. As the class hit a high note singing the word "sky," Jack leaned over and let the huge wad of gum drop from his mouth into his moistened hand. Then he began applying the gum to the underside of the folding desktop, just as he'd planned.

He stuck it first to the front outside edge and then pulled a heavy smear toward the opposite corner. Then he stretched the mass to the other corner and repeated the action, making a big, sticky X. Round and round Jack dragged the gum, working inward toward the center like a spider spinning a gooey, scented web.

As the bell rang Jack stood up and pulled the last gob of gum downward, pasting it onto the middle of the metal seat. A strand of sagging goo led upward, still attached to the underside of the desk.

It was the perfect crime.

The whole back of the music room reeked of artificial watermelon. And that gob on the seat? Sheer genius. Jack allowed himself a grim little smile as he shouldered his way into the hall.

There were two more class periods, so a kid would *have* to notice the mess today—this very afternoon. Mr. Pike would have to pull the desk aside so no one would get tangled in the gunk. Mr. Pike would need to get *someone* to clean it up before tomorrow.

So after *someone* had swept the rooms and emptied the trash cans and washed the chalkboards and dusted the stairs and mopped the halls and cleaned the entryway rugs, *someone* would also have to find a putty knife and a can of solvent and try to get a very sticky, very smelly desk ready for Tuesday morning. It would be a messy job, but *someone* would have to do it.

And Jack knew exactly who that someone would be. It would be the man almost everyone called John—John the janitor.

Of all the kids in the school, Jack was the only one who didn't call him John. Jack called him a different name.

Jack called him Dad.

---

## Chapter 2

# WhAT DO YoU WAnt to Be?

Ordinarily, no one would have imagined that Jack Rankin would vandalize a desk. But this was not an ordinary school year for Jack—or for any of his classmates, either.

The town of Huntington was growing, and more families with kids were moving in all the time. The town seemed to be playing a game of musical chairs—too many kids and not enough schoolrooms.

The kids in grades nine through twelve were all set. They had already made the move to a brand-new high school out on the west edge of town. The elementary school was still in good shape, but it was only big enough now for the kids in kindergarten through grade three.

It was Jack and the other kids caught in the middle grades who had the problem. The old junior high would work fine for grades four and five—that is, after about ten months of repair work. And the kids in grades six, seven, and eight would have a shiny, new junior high school—in about another year.

So where do you park Jack and about seven hundred other kids and all their teachers and textbooks and computers and printers and copiers and TVs and VCRs and art supplies, plus their library, for a whole school year?

Simple. You put them in the old high school.

Not simple. Not simple at all.

The old high school was . . . well, it was old.

The four-story brick building had been part of Huntington's town center for more than seventy-five years. The broad front lawn was split by a wide sidewalk leading up to the front steps. High above the front steps, a square bell tower rose another thirty feet beyond the roofline. The bell tower was capped by a green copper dome with a weather vane on top—made in the shape of an open book.

The old high school had been built back when fewer kids went on to college. It was Huntington's monument to higher education. For generations graduation from Huntington High had been the goal line.

But not for Jack and the other middle graders.

For them it was going to be an educational stopover—sort of like a long field trip. It would be nothing more than a strange world they would pass through on their way to somewhere else.

And from the second Jack heard about the move, he wished he could make the whole place just disappear.

The news of the school changes had been mailed to every home in Huntington just before spring break during Jack's fourth-grade year. His mom had read the letter aloud at supper one night.

Someone at the school superintendent's office thought it would be fun to give the transition process a cute name. The letter began like this:

*Dear Student:*
*Are you and your friends and family ready*
*for Huntington's newest adventure in learning?*
*Next year will be the year of*
*THE BIG SWITCHEROO!*

Jack was not amused.

After she finished the letter, his mom said, "Don't you think it's exciting, Jack? Those special tours in June should be fun. They want all the kids to feel comfortable, especially the fourth- and fifth-grade kids. . . . Of course, that's not a problem for you, I mean with your dad working there and all."

Jack looked quickly at his dad across the dinner table. "Won't you be going to work at the new high school, Dad? I mean, you're the high school janitor, right?"

Wiping his mouth, John Rankin smiled and said, "Nope. It doesn't work that way. What I am is the janitor for a *building*. The high school and all the high school kids are moving, but the building stays—so I stay too. No one knows that building like I do. Unless the town decides to tear it down, that'll be where I work."

Jack's mom said, "I loved going to school in that old place. It's got character, you know? And Jackie, if you don't want to take the bus some mornings, you could ride to school in the pickup with your dad."

Looking down at the pile of peas on his plate, Jack thought, *Yeah, right. Like I'm going to ride to school with the janitor.*

Jack knew he'd be on that bus every day, no matter what.

Jack remembered the first time he had been asked about his future. It was second grade, and Miss Patton had a let's-get-acquainted session on the first day of school. Jack liked Miss Patton. She wore the same kind of perfume that his grandmother wore, only a lot less. She was conducting a little public interview with each student. She asked questions like, Do you have any brothers or sisters? Do you have any pets? What's your favorite food? Do you like sports? If you could go anywhere in the world, where would you go?

The last question she asked was always, And what do you want to be when you grow up?

The answers to that question had been all over the place.

"I'm going to be a policeman."

"I want to be a doctor."

"I want to own a ranch and raise cows and chickens."

"I want to be a lawyer when I grow up."

"I'm going to be an astronaut and fly to Jupiter."

"I'm going to make computers."

Then it was Jack's turn.

Favorite color? Blue.

Brothers or sisters? One little sister.

Favorite food? Pizza.

"And what do you want to be when you grow up, Jack?"

There was no hesitation. Jack smiled with perfect second-grade certainty and he said, "I want to be a janitor, like my dad."

Before Miss Patton could say something like,

"That's great, Jack," some kids in the class began to giggle. Raymond Hollis blurted out, "A janitor? That's a job for dum-dums! Hey, Jack wants to grow up to be a dum-dum like his dum-dum daddy!"

That got the whole class laughing. Miss Patton shushed them and said, "Raymond, that was not nice, and you owe Jack an apology. Being a janitor is a perfectly good job, and I'm sure Jack is very proud of his dad."

Jack *was* proud of his dad, and he loved him very much. But laughter from kids is more powerful than words from teachers. Raymond had to stand up and say, "I'm sorry, Jack," but Jack could tell he didn't mean it.

Ever since that day in second grade, whenever the conversation turned toward parents and jobs, Jack clammed up.

But as fifth grade approached, the topic was going to be unavoidable. All summer long, whenever Jack thought about school, he felt like he was trapped in a bad dream.

## Chapter 3

# L Is for Loser

On his first day of fifth grade Jack had kept a lookout for his dad. He only saw him once, across the crowded cafeteria, leaning on a push broom by the main doorway. He was wearing his usual work clothes—dark green pants and a matching shirt with his name stitched in red letters on a white patch above the pocket. His dad smiled and waved. Jack barely nodded, and then looked away. He ate his lunch in a hurry and left through the side hallway door.

During the rest of September, Jack saw his dad once or twice a day. Usually they were both busy, both going somewhere in a hurry. It was like they lived in parallel universes. They passed through the same time and space without ever actually meeting. The arrangement suited Jack just fine.

Then on Monday afternoon, the fifth of October, disaster struck.

Jack was sitting in math class. Mrs. Lambert

was reviewing how to add fractions with different denominators. Two seats away, in the front row, Lenny Trumbull's stomach had a disagreement with the cafeteria ravioli. The ravioli won. Without warning, Lenny spread his lunch all over the green linoleum floor.

Mrs. Lambert hurried Lenny down to the nurse's office, and she sent Rick Arneson to get the janitor.

To escape the smell and avoid the vomit-o-domino effect, the whole math class was crowded into the back of the room by the open windows. Jack had gotten there first and practically had his whole head out the farthest window. Fortunately for his sensitive nose, the airflow was coming into the room instead of out of it. The breeze was from the direction of downtown, and Jack could smell the fries and hamburgers cooking at the diner seven blocks away.

Keeping his place by the window, Jack turned slightly and watched the doorway. There were always one or two other janitors in the building besides his dad. It didn't have to be John. Rick could find someone else. It didn't have to be John.

But it was. Jack's dad showed up with a bucket, a mop, a plastic bag of red sawdust, and a dustpan and brush. Jack cringed. He quickly ducked behind a knot of girls and turned to look out the window.

The rest of the class watched the janitor with horrified fascination. First, John shook out a few cups of sawdust to soak up the liquid. After a minute he swept the whole soggy mess into the dustpan and took it right out into the hallway. Then he shot some ammonia over the damp spot from a sprayer he pulled from his belt, and then swabbed the entire area down with the fresh mop. The smell was completely gone.

Mrs. Lambert had returned, and from the back of the room she said, "Thanks a lot, John."

John Rankin nodded and said, "All in a day's work."

Mrs. Lambert said, "All right, back to your seats, everyone. Show's over." The kids began moving toward their desks.

As John the janitor pushed the rolling bucket toward the door he glanced up and saw Jack. His face broke into a big smile.

And then he said it: "Hi, son."

Jack mumbled, "Hi," and then looked down, pretending to search for something in his notebook.

As his dad walked out into the hallway that Monday afternoon Jack felt like a giant letter had been branded on his forehead—*L*, for Loser.

Jack sat down, his ears burning red.

It was Kirk who struck first.

Kirk Dorfmann was a walking fashion ad. From shoes to cap he was a billboard of logos and trademarks—all the very latest clothes, all very expensive. Kirk grinned and leaned across the aisle toward Jack. In a voice loud enough for most of the class to hear he said, "Hey, does Daddy let you push the big broom sometimes, Jackie? Oh, I forgot—you have to get a special permit to drive one of those things. Nice outfit he's wearing today. Your dad looks great in green polyester."

It had been a long time since Jack had punched anyone. In his mind an iron fist formed, and he could feel it slamming into Kirk's soft, fleshy smirk. Jack could feel the teeth behind the lips giving way as he followed through with his full weight.

But before thought could become action, Mrs. Lambert slipped between the two boys. Her eyes flashed, and she said, "Kirk, I'll see *you* after class."

Mrs. Lambert moved back into the math lesson, and it seemed like things had returned to normal.

But they hadn't, not for Jack.

Jack sat smoldering through the rest of the class. His jaw ached from gritting his teeth. He ignored Mrs. Lambert and passed the last fifteen minutes

16

imagining how he'd get back at Kirk. He knew Kirk would never fight him. Jack had a reputation in that department. *Just let me get him alone down by the locker room*, thought Jack. *I'll mop the floor with him!* Jack said those words to himself and immediately got even angrier that he would choose that particular way to describe winning a fight.

When class ended, Jack hoped for a clean getaway, but the door clogged up with chatting girls, and the hallway was jammed with seventh graders coming back from their lunch period. Kirk went up to Mrs. Lambert's desk, and Jack edged toward the door and got in front of Marla Jenkins and Sue Driscoll. He wanted to be far enough away to be able to pretend he couldn't hear what Mrs. Lambert said to Kirk. It was just a scolding anyway, stuff about respect for others. Jack was still ten feet from the doorway when Kirk rejoined his buddy, Luke Karnes.

Luke was one of Kirk's trendy little group. Luke looked as if he followed Kirk around the Mall of America, taking notes on exactly what Kirk bought and how he put his fashion costumes together. Tall, thin, and long-legged, Luke was always a step or two behind Kirk, always trying to catch up, always trying to impress him. Luke started talking to Kirk, pretending that Jack couldn't hear him.

"Hey, Kirk, must take a lot of talent to clean up a bunch of puke, huh? Sure wish *I* could learn how to do that."

Kirk said, "Well, just forget about it, Luke. It's a gift, y'know? And you have to go to a special janitor's college and take a course in vomit wiping before you can even try it. Only a few special people ever learn how to do it right—and it's passed on with pride from father to son." Kirk paused, then in a voice dripping with sarcasm he said, "I sure wish *my* dad was a janitor!"

"Yeah," said Luke, "me, too!"

Jack kept his eyes straight ahead, his lips pressed together. Marla and Sue giggled as Kirk and Luke finished their little routine, and if Mrs. Lambert heard what they'd said, she pretended she hadn't.

Jack finally made it into the hallway. He bolted left toward his locker. As he got to the corner he glanced over his shoulder at Kirk and Luke, his eyes flashing with hatred. It was the wrong moment to look backward.

John Rankin had just rinsed his mop and refilled the rolling bucket at the utility closet in the fifth-grade hall. At the exact moment Jack was rounding the corner at an angry run, his dad was coming the other way with the bucket.

The collision was spectacular. The bucket didn't

tip all the way over, but the force of Jack's impact knocked the mop out onto the floor with a clatter that made everyone in the hallway turn and stare. Jack lost his footing in the water that sloshed onto the floor. His math book and papers went flying, and Jack skidded to a stop against the lockers, sitting in a puddle.

Led by Kirk and Luke, the hallway erupted into laughter and clapping.

John rushed over to his son. "You all right, Jack?" He tried to take Jack by the elbow and help him up. Jack jerked his arm away, not even looking at his dad. Ignoring the wet worksheets and his scattered homework papers, Jack scrambled to his feet, grabbed his math book, stepped around his dad, and hurried down the hall. The laughter died out amid the normal sounds of a few hundred kids passing classes. Jack jerked open his locker, grabbed his social studies book, kicked the door shut, and headed downstairs.

Six minutes later Jack was sitting on a stool in the art room at a worktable by himself. He pounded and pushed at the lump of reddish clay in front of him, both fists clenched.

Jack stared at the clay, replaying his humiliation again and again. Inside him a firestorm roared and hissed. It was impossible to keep it in.

So all of Jack's churning anger shot straight up through the art-room ceiling, a flaming tornado of hurt and embarrassment.

It hurtled through the halls of the old high school, smacking into lockers, crashing down stairwells, vaporizing doors and windows and walls.

And when his anger had reached maximum force and speed, it needed a target.

Kirk? A major annoyance, but hardly worth a full attack.

Luke? A total dweeb—not even on the radar screen.

Like a guided missile packed with deadly resentment, Jack's anger homed in on the ultimate target, the true cause of his problems, and at last it burst into hot crimson fragments above the unsuspecting head of John the janitor.

The sizzling chunks of Jack's burning rage stuck to his father—like gobs of well-chewed watermelon bubble gum.

Chapter 4

# The Sweet Smell of Victory

Sitting in English class with his heart pounding away, Jack reviewed the mission.

Just five minutes ago he had delivered a crushing blow to the enemy, a major assault—gummage in the first degree.

His music-room attack was undetected, the weapon was untraceable, and the result was unbelievably messy.

The only flaw was that Jack would not be able to watch his dad's face when he saw that desk. *If only I could be there,* he thought. *I could point at the desk and say, "Okay, Janitor John—janitor this!" Or maybe I'd say, "Go ahead, work your magic, Tidy Guy. You decided to go and become Mr. Clean—so here's a little present from your number one fan!"*

Jack grinned, savoring the imagined moment.

"Well, Jack? What is it?"

Uh-oh—battle stations. It was Mrs. Carroll in a

lime green pantsuit, bearing down from the front left flank. Artillery fire had already begun.

Jack straightened up in his chair, frantically scrolling through that tiny part of his brain that had been tracking the teacher, trying to recall her last two or three droning sentences. Something about parts of speech, something about—and in a flash he knew, like instant replay in his head. With the sweetest smile he could manage he said, "It's a preposition, right?"

Mrs. Carroll glared at him and edged a little closer. She'd been watching him from the corner of her eye for the past thirty seconds, and she could have sworn Jack Rankin was completely zoned out. Daydreaming was her pet peeve, and this was the fifth time she had tried—and failed—to catch Jack at it. Pursing her lips, she said, "Yes, the word *across* is a preposition." Her eyes narrowed and she edged half a step nearer. Mrs. Carroll reminded Jack of a green lizard getting ready to flip its tongue out to snap up a fly. She said, "Now, use it in a sentence."

The sentence that popped into Jack's head was, "The English teacher darted across the ceiling like a chameleon," but what he said was, "The fisherman paddled his canoe across the lake."

Lizard Woman glared at Jack an extra second or

two. She wanted to be sure he got the message that he had almost been a very dead fly.

"Yes," she said. "That's fine." Whirling away, she instantly settled on a new victim. "Jessie, in the sentence Jack just made up, what word is the *object* of the preposition?"

Surviving a direct hit from the reptile patrol was a little scary, so Jack assigned another tenth of his mind to the unpleasant job of watching out for Mrs. Carroll.

Glancing at the clock, Jack saw he had another thirty minutes of eighth period to go. With an inward smile he went back to his own thoughts, replaying his secret victory again and again—and Jack especially enjoyed thinking about that desk, sitting there like a sweet, sticky time bomb in the back row of the music room.

## Chapter 5

# School Justice

Mr. Pike reported the ruined desk to the office over the music-room intercom at the start of eighth period. Mr. Ackerby dropped what he was doing and hurried upstairs to take a look. He liked detective work, especially when the trail was fresh. The vice principal was on the case.

Looking at the desk with Mr. Pike, Mr. Ackerby shook his head. Then, just to be polite, he asked, "So, Dave, got any suspects for me?" Mr. Pike seemed like he was always in his own wacky little music zone, so Mr. Ackerby didn't expect him to be much help.

"Absolutely," said Mr. Pike. "Got it all figured out."

Mr. Ackerby's eyebrows shot up. "Really?" Like Jack, Mr. Ackerby didn't understand that a good choral director notices everything.

Mr. Pike nodded and said, "Clear as a bell. I've got fifty-six kids in that seventh-period class, and three on the absence list today, so fifty-three were here. I make the kids fill the room from front to back, and there are fifty-one chairs in the first four rows. I always look up to see who's late when the bell rings, and today Kerry Loomis and Jack Rankin were almost tardy. They had to be the only kids sitting in the last row today. I wouldn't think either of them would do this, but they were back there. I'm sure of that."

As he returned to the office Mr. Ackerby revised his opinion of Mr. Pike. Then he looked up the class schedules for Loomis, Kerry, and Rankin, Jack.

Five minutes later Mr. Ackerby had a quick conversation with the Loomis girl in the hallway outside her social studies class. Mr. Ackerby could tell she was innocent.

So it had to be the Rankin boy.

Someone was about to learn that there is no such thing as the perfect crime—especially at school. And he was going to learn it the hard way.

About twenty minutes into eighth period Mr. Ackerby appeared at the doorway of Jack's English class. He said, "Excuse me, Mrs. Carroll—I need to have a word with Jack Rankin."

Jack knew.

He knew why Mr. Ackerby wanted to talk with him.

As if in a fog, Jack got up from his desk and walked through the silent room, his face chalky white, his mouth dry.

One look and Mr. Ackerby was sure he had his man.

Mr. Ackerby closed the door to the classroom and glared down into Jack's pale face. Jack couldn't look him in the eye. Without raising his voice, Mr. Ackerby said, "Jack, I'd like you to walk down to the music room and bring a folding desk back to my office for me."

Jack gulped. Weakly, lamely, hopelessly, he asked, "Which desk?"

Mr. Ackerby's eyes flashed, and he said, "Hold out your hands."

Jack raised his hands up to about his waist, and Mr. Ackerby said, "Higher, and palms up." Leaning forward, Mr. Ackerby sniffed the left hand, and then the right one.

Watermelon.

Pointing at Jack's right hand, he said, "Bring me the desk that smells like *that.*"

It was a long way to the music room. Jack was tempted to dash down the stairway and out the door and just keep running and running. But he knew he couldn't.

Mr. Pike was rehearsing with the seventh-grade

chorus. He looked up from his music stand when Jack came in. He shook his head and gave Jack a frown, but he didn't miss a beat. Jack grabbed the desk and made his way awkwardly back out the door.

As he walked to the office Jack's mind filled with images of the horrors to come. By the time he arrived at Mr. Ackerby's doorway, the desk seemed to weigh about three hundred pounds.

Mr. Ackerby was sitting on a bookcase by the window in his office, waiting. Pointing with a stubby index finger, he showed where he wanted the desk and motioned Jack into a chair. Then he walked over and tipped the folding desk onto its side so they could both get a good look at the incredible mess on the bottom. The office filled up with the heavy scent of the gum.

Mr. Ackerby shook his head. "Look at that! Unbelievable! What in the *world* could you have been thinking? Tell me, Jack. What *were* you thinking?"

Mr. Ackerby had not had time to read Jack's school record, so he didn't know that Jack was a pretty good student and had never been in any real trouble at the elementary school.

At this moment all Mr. Ackerby knew was that this kid in blue jeans and a black T-shirt had worked pretty hard to destroy a desk. And whenever he caught someone damaging property, Mr. Ackerby didn't have to pretend to be angry. It was the real thing.

Jack looked steadily at the man's brown necktie and tried not to flinch. Jack could smell the man's shampoo, his shaving cream, his aftershave lotion, the ham-and-mustard sandwich he had eaten for lunch, and the mint he was sucking on.

Jack was angry at his dad, and he was angry at himself, and he hated the way things were spinning out of control. He clenched his jaw and worked very hard to keep his eyes from filling with tears.

Jack had been asked a question, and Mr. Ackerby didn't like waiting. He leaned forward and spoke even louder. "I *demand* an answer, young man. Look at this mess! What *were* you thinking?"

Jack glanced at the desk, then into Mr. Ackerby's squinty eyes, and then back to his ugly necktie. Jack couldn't quite explain that question to himself, not clearly, and there was no way he was going to open up and try to explain all his feelings to this guy.

So Jack said, "I don't know. I just . . . I just did it."

As if he could not believe what he was hearing,

Mr. Ackerby bent his face down close to Jack's and repeated, "You 'just did it'? Well, you know what, buddy boy? You're going to just UN-did it!"

He turned on his heel, and after a couple of quick steps sat down at his desk with a *thump*. Mr. Ackerby grabbed a pen and began writing a note on a stationery pad. He finished it, ripped it off, sealed it in an envelope, and began writing again. He said, "I'm sending a note home to your parents, and I'll be putting a memo in your permanent file. And starting today, you can cancel all your after-school plans."

Mr. Ackerby ripped the second piece of paper off the notepad, sealed it in another envelope, then stood up and walked over to Jack. Handing him the first envelope, he said, "This is for you to take home to your parents. Get it signed, bring it back tomorrow."

Turning around, he nudged the desk with the toe of his brown shoe. "You take this ruined desk down to the janitor's workshop in the basement by the boys gym. Then get back to your class." Mr. Ackerby paused, and handed Jack the second envelope. "Immediately after school you go back to the workshop and you hand *this* envelope to the chief custodian, and you tell him that you have volunteered for after-school gum patrol—an hour a day—for the next three weeks. Now get going."

School justice, exactly the way Mr. Ackerby liked it—swift and certain.

As Jack lugged the smelly desk through the empty hallways and then down the stairs into the workshop, he was praying no one would be there—and no one was. He set the desk in the middle of the room and ran back up the stairs. He got to his English class just as the bell was ringing. He copied the assignment off the board, picked up his books, and went to social studies.

All during ninth period Jack fretted and worried. He wondered how much his dad would yell at him. He wondered if his mom would ground him. He wondered if something like this in his file would keep him from playing football when he got to high school. And he wondered if Mr. Ackerby had any idea that "the chief custodian" was his dad.

Jack felt stupid for getting caught, and even worse, now he'd have to be the junior janitor for three whole weeks. There was no way out. If anyone in the school hadn't figured out that John the janitor was his dad, they wouldn't be left out of the secret for long.

And of course, there was only one person to blame for the whole mess. Jack clenched his teeth and pressed his lips together, barely containing an urge to spit. And he thought, *Thanks again,* Dad.

## Chapter 6

# Reporting for Duty

People said Jack looked like his dad, and he hated it. They said it often enough that Jack guessed it was true. Sure, he could see that they both had straight brown hair parted near the middle, and the same thick eyebrows that almost touched above the same deep-set brown eyes. Jack was a little taller than about half the other fifth-grade kids. He guessed he was on track to end up about the same height as his dad, just under six feet, and he already had the same strong arms and broad shoulders. Even Jack's real name was the same—John Philip Rankin Jr.

But the likeness went deeper than that, deeper than Jack liked to admit. It was more than the lines cut by a strong chin or a straight nose, more than a certain smile or a way of walking or a pattern of speech.

Like his dad, Jack was mostly quiet and thoughtful. He was happy to be on his own, but he could also be friendly and quick to smile. He wasn't shy, but when he spoke, he spoke carefully.

There was a steadiness about Jack most of the time—unless you got on his bad side. Jack didn't get mad easily, and neither did his dad. But when either of them *did* get mad, look out.

And as Jack went to find his dad after school he was ready for the worst.

Jack stopped on the metal stairs leading down to the shop. The shop was next to the boiler room, so it was always cozy down there during the cold months. The main boiler was running now, and the roar of the burner made the stairs tremble beneath Jack's feet. The air coming up past him was loaded with different smells, workshop smells. The air was warm, but it didn't seem cozy, not today.

Jack set his face into a hard "Who cares?" sort of look. He took a deep breath and started down the stairs.

Halfway down, Jack let out a sigh of relief. The place was empty. The folding desk was still sitting in the middle of the gray concrete floor, right where he had left it earlier. Dim afternoon sunshine from the window well on the far wall made a small patch of light on the floor. The only other light came from the lamp on his dad's desk.

Mr. Ackerby had told him to go to the shop after school, and here he was. Jack thought, *It's not my fault if Mr. Big-Shot Janitor is busy somewhere else.* So Jack crossed the workshop to his dad's desk and sat down.

Jack tipped back in the old swivel chair and slowly spun it around. As he did he looked up at the bookshelves mounted on the wall behind the desk. He didn't remember seeing them before. A row of binders on the top shelf caught his eye. Each notebook was carefully labeled. PLUMBING LOG, ROOFING SCHEDULE, GROUNDSKEEPING, BOILER MAINTENANCE, SUPPLIES & EQUIPMENT, PURCHASING, ALARM & BELL SYSTEMS, FIRE CONTROL SYSTEMS, ELECTRICAL SYSTEM—there were more than a dozen binders. The lower shelf was jammed with fat catalogs from suppliers, some of them twice as thick as the Yellow Pages.

One catalog was labeled LEWIS BROTHERS—POWER EQUIPMENT. Jack loved tools, and he was good at making things, fixing things. His dad had got him his own toolbox for Christmas when he was seven, and he'd been gradually filling it with tools—real ones, not kids' tools.

Jack stood up to reach for the tool catalog when suddenly the room flooded with fluorescent light. A booming voice said, "You looking for something?"

Jack turned around, startled, and the man halfway down the stairs saw his face. He grinned and said,

"Hey, it's Jackie boy! Look at the size of you—you must've picked up two inches since July! No wonder they sent you over to the high school this year."

Jack smiled and said, "Hi, Lou. Um . . . I've got to talk to my dad."

Lou chuckled as he came the rest of the way down to the shop. "Thought maybe you were some kid come here to check a book out of your daddy's library."

Lou Carswell was a tall, slender man with short-cropped hair and stooped shoulders. He and his wife had come to Jack's house for Sunday suppers and summer barbecues plenty of times. Lou had been working at the high school almost as long as John Rankin.

There was a poorly focused photo on his dad's dresser—four young guys in army uniforms. Jack knew one of them was his dad, and he was pretty sure one of them was Lou. He had never asked, but that's how it looked.

Lou said, "If you're waitin' for your dad, you got a long stretch ahead of you. He's up on three west in the science lab, fixing a motor in the ventilator. You'd best walk up there and find him."

Jack said, "No . . . it's okay. I can wait."

Lou shook his head and motioned toward the stairs with his thumb. "I'm not kiddin', Jackie—he's probably got another forty minutes of work on that unit, so just pick up and get up there to room 336 right now—go on. He'll be glad to see you."

With the note from Mr. Ackerby weighing him down, Jack started the long hike to the third floor, palms sweating, mouth dry. He trudged up the stairs like a convict headed for the gallows.

Jack could have found his way just by following his nose. He had noticed a strange electrical smell all over the school right after lunch. As he approached room 336 the sharp odor of burned wiring got stronger and stronger. Peeking in the doorway, Jack saw his dad bent over the ventilator by the windows, his left arm completely inside the casing. He was reaching for something. Vent covers and spools of wire, nuts and bolts, pliers, wrenches, and wire clippers were spread out all over the floor and the nearest lab tables.

Taking a deep breath, Jack walked in and said, "Hi, Dad."

John Rankin turned his head. He smiled and said, "Hey, this is a surprise—good timing, too." He straightened up and pulled a flashlight from his back pocket. "I dropped a nut down behind the new motor assembly, and I can't get my hand in there to pick it up. Thought I was going to have to go all the way down to the shop and get a magnet. Here, I'm going to shine the light down from over this side, and you see if your hand can fit behind there and get it."

Jack thought, *What makes him think that I want to get all covered with grease and dirt like he is?* But Jack took a look down into the register, and then leaned way over, threaded his hand in, and came out with the nut. "Here."

"Great! That's going to save me some time." John Rankin straightened up and smiled at his son, and tossed him a rag to wipe off his hand. Looking into Jack's face for the first time, he saw right away this wasn't a social visit. In a quieter voice he said, "What's on your mind, Jack?"

Jack looked at the floor and said, "I . . . I got myself in some trouble, Dad." And he handed his father the note from Mr. Ackerby.

John pulled a chair out from under a lab table and sat down. He took his reading glasses from his shirt pocket and perched them on the end of his nose. Then he tore open the envelope, unfolded the paper, and started to read. Jack watched his face.

John Rankin read two lines and then looked up sharply at Jack, his dark eyebrows lifted in disbelief. "It was *you*? You're the one who messed up the desk that's down in the shop?" Jack reddened, but he met his father's eyes with a sullen look and nodded.

His dad looked back to the note. It only took him another ten seconds to finish it. He put the paper back in the envelope and laid it on the scarred black lab table. He took off his glasses and tucked them into his pocket. Then he turned his head and looked out the window. A brisk wind was pushing the fallen leaves into heaps along the fence around the football field.

John Rankin cleared his throat. "Hard to know what to make of this, son." There was a long pause, as if he hoped Jack would offer an explanation. Jack kept silent. Then John said, "But I guess there's time." He tapped the envelope on the lab table. "According to this, seems like we've got three weeks to get to the bottom of it."

John stood up and walked over to the ventilator. He looked in his toolbox and picked up a wrench, squinted at it to read the size, and then turned his back to Jack, both arms down inside the cabinet again. He said, "You know that door to the right of my desk down in the shop?"

Jack said, "Sure," and he thought, *What, does he think I'm a dummy?*

His dad continued, "Go inside and look on the shelves to the left. There's a can of special solvent called OFFIT that's pretty good with the fresh stuff. And you'll need a roll of paper towels and some rubber gloves and a stiff-bladed putty knife for the hardened gum. Toss your supplies in a plastic bucket to carry 'em around. Easier that way. And you'll need a trash bag. The buckets and the trash bags are behind the door to the right. After that folding desk is clean and back in the music room, you can move on to the tables and chairs in the library. I'll be checking your work, and I've got a feeling that Mr. Ackerby will too."

John turned around and tossed the wrench back into the toolbox. The metallic clatter made Jack jump. His dad said, "Any questions?"

"No."

"Then get to it."

John Rankin turned back to the broken ventilator, and Jack turned and headed back to the workshop for the third time today.

Jack felt so relieved he practically skipped down the empty stairway. His dad hadn't even yelled at him. Maybe it was a sign, a good omen. Maybe his mom wouldn't ground him. And maybe Ackerby would lighten up and let him off the hook after a week or so.

Who could say? Maybe gum patrol wasn't going to be so bad after all.

Then Jack caught himself. *What, am I nuts? Gum patrol not so bad? Yeah, right.*

## Chapter 7

# Gum Patrol

Jack got to the shop and gathered his supplies. The folding desk was waiting for him.

Jack turned the desk upside down on the workshop floor and bent over to take a careful look, poking here and there with his finger. His research had been right on target. Fresh watermelon Bubblicious was very sticky, very disgusting.

Jack stood up, clenched his jaw, and gave the desk a swift kick. This was *supposed* to be his dad's job. Still, Jack was smart enough to appreciate the irony of getting stuck in his own trap, so he heaved a big sigh, turned the underside of the desk toward the light, and went to work.

Jack launched his attack with the putty knife. Big mistake. The gum was too fresh. It smeared around, covering more of the surface. It took him five minutes to clean the blade of the putty knife, and when he was done, he had to shake his hand until the tool clattered to the floor, its black plastic handle fouled with crimson.

Then Jack crumpled up a paper towel and tried rubbing. The paper ripped to shreds. It added a layer of sticky white fiber on the goo, like grass clippings blown onto fresh road tar.

Finally, he tried putting two layers of paper towel around the end of the putty knife. Pushing with the covered end of the blade, he was able to plow up a ridge of gum. Then he could close the paper towel around the glob and pull it off. The threads created by pulling off wads of gum fell onto the workshop floor. The mess kept spreading to a wider and wider area.

Gob after strand after wad, Jack scraped and pulled and rubbed until, twenty minutes later, only a massive smear was left.

Time for the solvent. Jack read the directions on the can and then poured some OFFIT onto a folded paper towel and started to rub. The gum dissolved as if by magic, staining the paper towel crimson but leaving a clean surface behind. Inch by inch, Jack rubbed and rubbed until the job was done.

The desk was no longer sticky, gooey, or smelly, but Jack was another story. There was gum on the front and back of both hands, and bits of paper towel were stuck between his fingers. There were thin strands of gum crisscrossing his shoes and shoelaces. Both knees of his jeans had crimson spots, and there was a glob the size of a pea stuck in the hair of his right eyebrow.

Carefully reading the OFFIT label again, Jack made sure it was safe to use the solvent on himself. In another few minutes he had got most of the gum off his hands and shoes and pants. The can said to keep the liquid away from eyes, so Jack just picked and pulled at the gum in his eyebrow until he'd got most of it out. It still felt funny, but when he looked at his face in the mirror over the utility sink, he could see only a trace of crimson. Good enough for now.

Jack stuffed the sticky paper towels into a trash barrel by the stairs. Then he took the clean desk back to the music room, and had to find Lou to have him open the door. On the way back he stopped at his locker to get his backpack and coat, and finally ran back to the workshop to put the equipment away.

It was 3:25, and today's hour of gum patrol was officially over.

Jack ran up the workshop stairs, streaked down the hallway toward the back door, and just barely got onto the last late bus. Dropping onto a squeaky seat as the bus lurched out of the parking lot, Jack was panting, but relieved.

If he had missed this bus, it would have caused other problems. He would have had to hang out for at least another hour and ride home with his dad, something he didn't want to do, not ever—and especially not today.

If he had ridden home with his dad, then the *other* note from Mr. Ackerby would have been delivered to both his parents at once. Jack was pretty sure things would go better if his mom read the note first, all by herself.

At least, that's what he hoped.

## Chapter 8

# HUNG JURY

Mrs. Rankin got home from work at four fifteen every day, so Jack was cutting it close. He ran the half block from the bus stop, let himself in, and hung up his coat and backpack in the front closet. He could tell by sniffing that his mom wasn't home yet and that dinner hadn't been started.

Jack dashed into the living room and struck a quick deal with his little sister. "Listen, Lois. Don't tell Mom I got home so late today, okay? And don't tell her I forgot to call Mrs. Genarro. It's worth a dollar if you keep your mouth shut, okay?"

If Jack missed the bus, he was supposed to call their neighbor so she could keep a lookout for Lois.

His sister didn't take her eyes off the TV. She asked, "Is it worth a dollar fifty?" Lois was in third grade. She thought her parents made too big a deal about her life after school. But now and then it was useful to have everyone worried about her.

Jack gritted his teeth. "Fine. A dollar fifty." He

didn't have time to haggle, and he didn't need another issue, not right now, not just before a trial.

A minute later the station wagon pulled into the driveway, a door slammed at the garage on the alley, and Mom was at the kitchen door, her huge purse over one arm and a bag of groceries in the other. Jack was down the steps in no time, being helpful.

"Thanks, Jackie. Put the ice cream in the freezer right away, would you? And the milk needs to be put away too." His mom came up the stairs behind him, laid her coat over the back of a chair, and immediately pulled out a box of macaroni. "Put some water on to boil, will you, Jack? Use the deep saucepan."

"Mmmm . . . macaroni and cheese tonight?" asked Jack, reaching into the cabinet below the stove for the pan.

His mom nodded. "Yup." Then she added with a smile, "How'd you guess?"

Jack grinned back. "Just a genius."

Things were going well. A little helpfulness, a little humor.

Jack knew all about timing. In a case like this timing was everything. Now was the right moment, because at the first real pause in the flow his mom would ask that dreaded question, "What happened at school today?" He had to tell her before she asked, so it wouldn't look like he had been trying to hold something back. A point for helpfulness, a point for cheerfulness, a point for being honest about bad news. Jack needed all the points he could get.

Mrs. Rankin sat down at the table with her recipe box, looking for her old baked macaroni and cheese recipe. Jack took notice. Sitting down is good, more relaxed.

Jack quickly slipped into the chair next to her and said, "Mom, I got in some trouble at school today. I got caught sticking gum on the bottom of a desk. I know it was wrong, and I'm being punished for it. I've got a note for you and Dad from the vice principal." He handed her the note.

One clean, smooth action. A brief introduction, a complete confession, a dash of sorrow, and a short explanation. Jack hoped his opening remarks would lessen the impact of Mr. Ackerby's note. The man had only taken about a minute to write it—how bad could it be?

Lois had a built-in radar for drama. The show in the kitchen was a lot better than the one on TV. She crept silently to the doorway behind her mom and peered around the corner at Jack. She made a face and shook her finger at him, as if she were saying, *Naughty, naughty, naughty.* Jack glared at her, but Lois stayed put, a smug little smile on her face.

Mrs. Rankin broke the seal on the envelope. It was time for Exhibit A, the note.

Jack thought the jury would be sympathetic to his case. He was hoping he would get time off for good behavior.

Jack had underestimated Mr. Ackerby's talents as a writer.

As Mrs. Rankin scanned the note her lips pressed together into a thin line and her eyes narrowed.

Not good.

Then she read Exhibit A aloud:

*Dear Mr. and Mrs. Rankin:*

*I'm sorry to report that your son, Jack, did his best to ruin a desk today. In a deliberate act of vandalism he completely fouled the underside of a folding desk during his music class. The quantity of bubble gum he applied can only be described as enormous. His action required fore-thought and planning. It seems like an angry ges-ture to me. Yet when I asked him why he did it, he did not answer me. I will alert our counseling staff to this incident.*

*In the meantime, Jack will be required to stay after school one hour each day for the next three weeks. He will be helping our custodial staff clean gum off of furniture throughout the school.*

*Please call if you wish to discuss this matter further.*

*Sincerely,*
*Mr. Ronald Ackerby*
*Vice Principal, Huntington Middle School*

Helen Rankin did not explode. It took some doing, but she was too smart to get angry. Not about this. Anger would be the wrong response.

Helen wasn't angry, because she knew something that Mr. Ackerby didn't—at least, not yet. She knew that the "custodial staff" was headed up by Jack's dad, John Rankin.

She also knew her son. She knew this stunt was not about destroying property. She knew Jack hadn't done this just for kicks.

There was something else going on.

Helen Rankin had seen this coming, and here it was.

Jack was trying to get some clues from his mom's face after she'd read the note out loud. It was a tough call. Angry? Not quite. Sad? Yes, there was some sadness. But there was a whole bunch of other stuff going on that Jack couldn't pin down. He couldn't tell what was going to happen.

Helen Rankin spoke quietly, and all she said was, "Jack, I'm going to have to talk to your dad about this. You should go to your room and do homework until I call you for dinner."

Lois vanished from the doorway.

Jack said, "Okay, Mom." He pushed his chair back from the table, stood up, and walked out to the front closet to get his backpack.

It was the old go-wait-in-your-room situation. No decision. A hung jury. He headed up the stairs.

As Jack passed Lois's room she opened her door six inches, smiled sweetly, and stuck out her hand.

Jack thought, *Here I am, waiting on death row, and she wants her stinking dollar fifty!*

But there was something on Lois's palm. She batted her eyelashes, nodded down at her hand, and whispered, "Hey, Jack, want a piece of . . . *gum*?"

Lois got the door shut and locked just in time.

Jack put his face next to the door and hissed, "You are dead meat, funny girl."

Lois giggled and said, "I think I shall need *two* dollars. . . . Yes, two dollars will be enough. For now. But no coins—nice, crisp bills, please."

Jack kicked the bottom of her door and went down the hallway to his cell.

## Chapter 9

# Boy Territory

Jack's mom had known her husband since they went to Huntington High School together. Helen Parkman had first met John Rankin when he was in eleventh grade and she was in ninth. She had watched him catching touchdown passes for the Huntington Heralds during Friday-night football games. She had seen him at dances with his girl-friend, a cheerleader. She had seen him washing cars on Saturdays at his dad's used-car lot.

Helen Parkman had watched John Rankin from a distance. They knew each other, but they had never really been friends, not back then. John's family had some money, and they lived on the nicer side of town. Helen's family didn't. It was as simple as that. John Rankin was a golden boy, one of those kids "Most Likely to Succeed."

Then one day in the spring of 1967, just two months before his high school graduation, John Rankin disappeared. He had joined the army. It made quite a stir at Huntington High School. A lot of boys were getting drafted into the army because it was the middle of the Vietnam War. But no one was signing up for military service on purpose, not the infantry, and not for a four-year hitch. John had just turned eighteen, he had been accepted at a good college, and he might not have had to go into the service at all. There were savage pictures of the war on the evening news every day. It seemed like you'd have to be crazy to join the army.

It was a mystery back then. Why did he leave? When had he come back? How did he end up as the janitor at the high school?

Now Helen Rankin knew all the hows and whens and whys. Now she understood. And it all made perfect sense in the flow of her husband's life, in the long view.

But how could she help an eleven-year-old understand all that?

And how could she help her husband not feel hurt to learn that Jack was embarrassed—ashamed to have his classmates know his father was the school janitor?

Helen Rankin was a strong person. She had taken courses at the local junior college, and now she worked as a paralegal secretary for the town government. She had the respect of her co-workers and her boss. She took good care of her kids, and she and her husband made a good home for their family.

The only thing that made Helen feel helpless was this—being caught between her husband and her son.

She had a name for the feeling.

Helen Rankin was lost in Boy Territory.

When John Rankin's pickup pulled into the driveway at quarter of six, everybody in the house heard it.

For Jack it meant that the rest of his jury had arrived.

For his sister it meant that there would be more drama, more adventures in spying.

For his mom it meant that a delicate balancing act was about to begin.

Helen Rankin looked through the window over the sink. John didn't get out of the truck right away. When he did, he looked tired. She met him at the back door with a hug and a kiss.

He smiled and held her at arm's length. "So how's my best girl?"

She smiled back and said, "I've been better. I hear from Mr. Ackerby that you've got a new assistant for the next three weeks."

Helen hadn't been planning to bring up the subject so soon, but it seemed the most honest thing to do. No sense pretending they weren't both thinking about it.

Following his wife up the steps to the kitchen, John said, "That's a fact. Jack cleaned the desk he gummed up today. Took him most of an hour, but he did a good job. 'Course, the shop's a wreck, and I hate to think what his clothes are like. I've never seen such a mess."

John pulled out a chair and straddled it, his elbows on the seat back. Helen started peeling carrots at the sink. She asked, "Any idea why he did it?"

John pulled his note from Mr. Ackerby out of his shirt pocket and tapped it on the chair back. "Well, the vice principal says it was just vandalism, but I think there's more to it, don't you? And you know what? I helped Ackerby plan and organize that move all last summer, so you'd think he could put two and two together—I don't think that guy has it figured out that Jack's my son."

Helen kept peeling carrots, but turned and nodded toward the table. "I'm sure he doesn't know yet. That's the note . . . to the parents." Helen went to the refrigerator and got out a head of lettuce, glancing at John's face as he opened the second letter and started to read.

Turning back to the sink, she kept her voice even and asked, "What do you think? Is Mr. Ackerby right? Do you think Jack was angry?"

John Rankin didn't answer right away.

Helen wasn't sure what was coming. This was Boy Territory.

John started slowly. "Here's how I see it. We know Jack had to do it on purpose, and he knew a desk that messy would end up down in my shop. So I'm guessing that Jack's mad at me. It's been like he's wanted nothing to do with me for a long time. He hasn't said a word to me at school so far, not until last Monday."

Then John told Helen about cleaning up the floor and saying hi to Jack in his math class—and about the collision in the hall.

It was the perfect opening. Helen said, "John, I think Jack was very embarrassed by that. I think that solves the mystery."

John spoke slowly. "I know he was embarrassed by that fall in the hallway—but you mean he was embarrassed about *me*, right?"

Helen nodded.

There was an awkward silence. John said, "Makes sense. Smart, good-looking kid, and his old man's the janitor."

Another silence.

Then John said, "And thanks to Ackerby, now Jack's a janitor too. John Junior, the little janitor. He's really going to hate me now."

Helen turned around and said, "It'll all work out. You know Jack could never hate you, John."

John shook his head. "You'd maybe think different if you'd seen what he did to that desk." With some bitterness in his voice he added, "Of course, Jack doesn't stop and remember that he's never gone to bed hungry in his life, and that when he needs a new pair of shoes, there they are, just like magic. He's happy to have the money I make by cleaning up after people, isn't he?"

John stood up stiffly and walked to the side window. After a minute he said, "But there's no use getting mad about it. I just wish I knew what to do."

Helen wished the same thing. She said, "Well, you're going to see a lot more of each other during the next three weeks. It'll work out all right. I'm sure it will."

John Rankin hoped she was right.

## Chapter 10

# RUMORS

Jack couldn't believe it.

Dinner was a breeze. No yelling. No angry silences. His dad seemed a little quieter than usual, but that was about it. Jack kept quiet too.

There was some chitchat about school assignments and grades. Mom had some news about Aunt Mary and Uncle Bob driving up from Des Moines to visit at Thanksgiving. Ordinary dinner talk, with Mom doing most of the talking.

Lois was disappointed. She had been hoping for fireworks, a major scene with red faces and everybody spitting mad. Just once she wanted to see a big family blowup—with Jack as the target, of course. She stabbed her fork into the last piece of macaroni on her plate, ate it, drained her milk glass, and asked to be excused from the table.

As bedtime approached, Jack took inventory.

He wasn't grounded.

He still had full telephone privileges.

His allowance was intact.

Jack was pretty sure he could even get away without paying Lois her hush money.

It was almost like nothing had happened.

Jack was expecting a long, serious talk at bedtime, but it didn't happen. Mom said she was sure he had learned his lesson, and Jack said he was sure he had. She kissed him on the forehead, tucked the covers around him, said, "Sweet dreams," and shut his door.

Down the hall Jack heard his dad open Lois's door and say, "Good night, sweetheart." And he heard Lois say, "G'night, Daddy."

"Little Miss Perfect," Jack muttered.

Then Jack heard his dad's footsteps come toward his door. He thought, *Oh boy, here it comes.* He braced himself and quickly decided to pretend he was asleep.

The footsteps stopped. Then they began again, but his dad had turned around. Jack listened until his dad started down the stairs.

"That's fine by me," Jack said aloud to himself. "The last thing I need is a little sermon from the Broom King."

So the public part of Jack's long Monday ended.

But Jack's private day wasn't over. He lay awake for almost an hour.

Tuesday was coming. Jack looked at his alarm clock. The bus would arrive at his corner in exactly ten hours and twelve minutes—no, eleven minutes.

On Tuesday he'd have to go back to school.

Back to the scene of the crime.

Tuesday morning came right on schedule. The bus ride was uneventful, which was good. Jack needed to be on time so he could get rid of the letter his mom and dad had signed. He had to get it back to Mr. Ackerby.

Jack didn't go to his locker. He went right to the office, arriving there just as the sixth-grade buses were pulling up at the curb on Main Street. Jack chose that moment on purpose. He knew that Mr. Ackerby always met the morning buses out front.

He walked up to the school secretary's desk and said, "Excuse me. . . . Mr. Ackerby said I had to bring this letter back to him."

Mrs. Carter looked up from her computer screen, and her eyes flickered as she recognized him. "Oh . . . yes. Jack Rankin." Jack blushed a little.

She looked him in the face, trying to connect the story she'd heard with this polite young man standing in front of her desk. He certainly didn't look like a troublemaker to her. *Still,* she thought, *looks can be deceiving.*

Mrs. Carter held out her hand. "Mr. Ackerby's not here right now. Leave it with me, and I'll be sure he gets it."

Jack handed it to her with a polite smile, said, "Thank you," and left.

Easy as pie. Jack had passed the Note Return Test with flying colors.

It wasn't that he was afraid to meet up with Mr. Ackerby again. Jack just didn't see what good it would do. They would meet again, guaranteed. And whenever that was, that would be soon enough for Jack.

A school is like a small town. Even ordinary news travels fast.

But a really juicy story that involves crime and punishment can easily hit speeds of one or two hundred mouths an hour.

By eight forty-five on Tuesday morning the legend of Jack the Gummer was just hitting warp speed.

Jack's best friend was Pete Ramsey. The spelling of their last names had kept them sitting next to each other almost every year since kindergarten. This year they had the same homeroom and their lockers were side by side.

Jack had just pulled open the metal door when he noticed Pete. Pete had recently started wearing cologne, and Jack could always tell when he was in the area. Today Pete was also chewing gum— *Juicy Fruit,* Jack said to himself.

Without looking around, Jack said, "Hi, Pete."

There was no answer. Jack turned, and Pete was there, but he was just staring at him, his mouth open, gum on his tongue.

Pete said, "What are *you* doing here?"

"Uhh . . . standing at my locker?" asked Jack. "Is that the answer? Do I win the big prize?"

Pete was serious. "I thought you got expelled."

"Expelled?" said Jack. "What for?"

"For swearing at Mr. Pike during chorus and then sticking gum all over Mr. Ackerby's desk. Did you call Mr. Pike names—or what?"

Jack said, "Who told you all that?"

"It's everywhere," said Pete. "I heard it waiting in line down at the school store."

"Well, it's not true," said Jack. "All I did was stick a bunch of gum on the bottom of a folding desk—one desk. I got caught, and now I have to stay and clean off gum after school. That's all."

Pete said, "No swearing?"

"None," said Jack.

"No big fight with Mr. Ackerby?"

Jack shook his head. "Nope. He yelled at me, and he sent a note home to my folks, but I'm not even grounded."

The facts were pretty boring, and Pete lost interest immediately. As he began to dial his combination he shrugged. Then he said, "Hey, Little League registration is at the new high school gym this Saturday. You going?"

Jack leaned against the lockers and listened to Pete. He said "uh-huh" and nodded at the right moments, but he was thinking about the outrageous rumors.

Then, above Pete's chatter, Jack heard Luke using his best stage voice.

Luke said, "Hey, Kirk, look who's here! It's Gumbo."

Kirk Dorfmann's locker was across the hall. Kirk walked over, and Luke followed along.

Kirk said, "Yeah, you're right. It's Gumbo, son of Scumbo the Janitor. So, how's it going, Gumbo?"

Pete stepped between Jack and Kirk, his shoulders squared and fists clenched. With a sneer he said, "Hey look, Jack. It knows how to talk. I think its name is Tommy Polo Nautica. Run along now, Tommy Polo Nautica. You might get your nice yellow jacket all messed up."

Pete was not kidding, and Kirk knew it.

"Sure," said Kirk, "no problem. We were just leaving anyway—right, Luke? We want to go watch the janitor fold up the tables in the cafeteria."

Luke said, "Yeah, because he's so talented, y'know? See you guys later."

Pete and Jack watched them until they turned the corner at the end of the hallway.

"Dirtbags," said Pete.

"Yeah," said Jack. "Grade-A jerks. Thanks, Pete."


From what Pete had said about the rumors, Jack didn't know what to expect for the rest of the day.

But homeroom was normal, and the morning classes, too. Every once in a while Jack would notice a kid looking at him curiously. But when the rumor says you're expelled and you clearly are *not* expelled, reality wins.

Still, as he headed up the stairs after lunch Jack thought he saw two seventh-grade teachers giving him weird sideways glances. *Figures,* he thought. *Teachers gossip too.*


After school there was a note for Jack taped to the door of the supply closet in the workshop. It was from his dad.

*Jack—*

*Start on the tables and chairs in the library today. Mrs. Stokely is usually there after school, but if she's not, you can find Lou down near the auditorium, and Arnie is sweeping on two and three. I'll be fixing a toilet up on four if you need me.*

*Dad*

*Toilets,* thought Jack. *Great. My dad's in the toilet repair business.*

Jack pushed the door open and went into the supply closet. First, he got a fresh roll of paper towels. The putty knife, the solvent, and the rubber gloves were right where he had left them. Today he planned to use the rubber gloves.

Then he remembered his dad had said to use a bucket to carry stuff around. *Why not?* Jack thought. *After all, he's the big expert.*

Jack turned around to look on the other set of shelves. There were wet-mop heads and dust-mop heads, mop wringers, handle setups, big cans of liquid wax, two-gallon bottles of ammonia—but no buckets. Jack pulled the door out of the way and found what he needed: two stacks of buckets, metal and plastic.

Glancing up, Jack saw a gray wooden cabinet

hanging on the wall. It had been hidden behind the open door. Shallower than a medicine cabinet, it came out only about two inches from the wall. It was almost three feet wide and had hinges on either side so the doors could open out from the center. A hasp and a padlock held the cabinet doors shut.

It was an unusual padlock, the old kind— round, and made of solid brass, with rivets and a little flap on the side to cover the keyhole. Jack pushed the door of the closet out of the way to let the light shine on the lock.

As he took half a step forward to get a closer look Jack discovered something interesting.

The old brass lock was not snapped shut.

## Chapter 11

# Open Sesame

An open lock is a temptation for some people. For Jack it was more like an invitation. It wasn't like he was cracking a safe or robbing a bank. He was only interested in the lock—at first.

He pulled on it, and the curved shackle swung open on its pivot. Sliding the shackle out of the loop of the hasp, he turned toward the light to get a better look at the thing.

Cool and heavy in his hand, it was like a work of art. Jack flipped it over and read the words engraved on the back—THE CHAMPION LOCK COMPANY. And below the name was the patent date—1898! It was the kind of lock that stirs the imagination.

Turning back to the cabinet, Jack was all set to put the lock back just as he'd found it. But almost as an afterthought he flipped the latch off the doors and pulled on both at once.

There was a soft jingling, and as the doors opened wide so did Jack's eyes and mouth.

Keys.

They ran from the top left of the left-hand door to the bottom right of the right-hand door.

Row after row after row of keys.

Jack had found the key safe. Almost every big building has one. The cabinet held long rows of nails spaced far enough apart so keys could hang side by side and top to bottom without bumping. Each nail was tilted slightly upward so the keys would not fall off as the doors were opened and closed.

Each nail held at least one key, and some held as many as ten or twelve in little brass-and-silver stacks. On top of each pile there was a small, round identification tag.

Jack's eyes roamed over the stacks of keys, reading the tags. RM. 227, RM. 228, and so on; BOYS LCKR. RM.; ART SUPPL. CLOSET; CAFT. FREEZER; MAIN OFFICE.

Every classroom, every closet, every washroom, every office, every desk and cabinet and cupboard in the old high school had a lock, and every lock had a key, and every key was right there, staring Jack Rankin in the face.

His mind was reeling, and it's a credit to Jack's character that he didn't immediately begin to imagine some real crimes. It would have been so simple.

Jack sensed this. It made him uneasy.

He was about to close the doors, but then he thought,

*Hey, wait a second—I'm like a janitor now, right? And the janitor can have any keys he wants. I'll just consider this a little present from Ackerby and dear old Dad.*

Stepping in closer, Jack looked over the key tags again. Down near the lower right-hand corner he saw two stacks of keys, side by side. One was labeled BELL TOWER. The other was labeled STEAM TUNNEL.

For Jack these labels didn't suggest the chance to steal something, the chance to look up answers in a teacher's textbook, the chance to mess with the principal's computer or goof up the clock and bell system.

The attraction of these particular keys was much more powerful.

These keys suggested adventure.

BELL TOWER. No secret there. The tower on the high school ruled Huntington's tiny skyline. And finding it would be easy—just keep going up.

But STEAM TUNNEL? That was different. That was a mystery.

Jack thought, *What the heck is a steam tunnel anyway? And where would I look for one? And if I found it, where would it go?*

Carefully, suddenly alert to each small sound, Jack hooked the padlock onto the belt loop of his jeans. Then he used both hands to lift the stack of tower keys off its nail. There were seven keys in all, each one stamped with the number 501. Jack took the key from the bottom of the stack and then put the other six back on the board. He quickly repeated the process for the tunnel keys, taking the fifth one and replacing the remaining four. The tunnel keys were stamped with the number 73.

Stepping back with the two keys in his hand, Jack scanned the rows in the cabinet. No one would be able to tell that two little keys were missing, not just by looking. It was like borrowing two pebbles from a beach. *Borrowing,* Jack said to himself, *not stealing.*

Footsteps.

On the metal stairs.

Coming down into the shop.

Jamming the keys into the front pocket of his jeans, Jack closed the cabinet quickly, trying not to make anything jangle. He pulled the padlock from his belt loop and set it back in place, almost shut, just like it had been.

Grabbing a plastic bucket from the stack, he bumped into the metal pails on purpose. He tossed the can of OFFIT and the putty knife noisily into his bucket, grabbed the towels and gloves, and went out through the supply closet door just as Arnie reached the bottom of the stairs.

"Hi, Arnie," he said, smiling. His heart was pounding.

"Hey, Jack. Heard that I'd be seeing you around.

Got *stuck* with a little project, right?"

Arnie was a big joker, and he found himself very easy to amuse. He was a heavyset guy, and going up or down stairs made Arnie's face match his red hair and freckles. Laughing turned him a shade or two deeper. That much red made a striking contrast to the green collar of his work shirt.

Jack laughed too, mostly from relief. He was glad it hadn't been his dad coming to the shop. His dad might have noticed his uneasiness. Jack was not a good liar, and he felt like he was telling a lie by trying to act normal as he headed toward the stairs.

"That's a good one, Arnie. Yeah, I'm stuck all right. Well, got to get to work—see ya."

As Jack took the steps two at a time Arnie said, "Yup, time to *double your pleasure*—eh, Jackie?" But Jack was up the stairs and into the hallway, and Arnie was left laughing all by himself.

Jack headed for the library, up on the second floor, but gum was the last thing on his mind.

Swinging the bucket of supplies in his left hand, he reached into his pocket with the other one. Key number 501, key number 73.

He wasn't Jack the Gummer.

He wasn't Jack the janitor's son.

He was Jack the explorer.

Today, the tower; tomorrow—who knows?

## Chapter 12

# CHEWOLOGY

Jack's hour in the library was educational. When he knocked on her door at 2:35, Mrs. Stokely was bustling about behind the glass walls of her office. Smiling, she opened her door, looked him in the face, and immediately said, "You must be John's boy—and you must hear that a lot."

Jack nodded. "Yes, ma'am, I hear that pretty often. My name is Jack. . . . I . . . I'm supposed to start cleaning the gum off the bottoms of the chairs and tables."

The librarian's face darkened. Shaking her head, she said, "It burns me up, the way kids leave that stuff around." Then, smiling at Jack again, she said, "Well, it's sure nice of you to lend your dad a hand. If it weren't for his help, I'd have never got this place ready for the opening of school. And I've still got plenty to do, believe you me!"

Jack didn't correct Mrs. Stokely's misunderstanding about why he was working. Instead he nodded and said, "Well . . . better get busy."

The high school library was a big room. Fourteen large wooden tables ran in two rows down the center of the space. The old card catalog stood on massive cast-iron legs to the left of the circulation desk. There were three computer terminals on top of it now, their screens dark except for blinking cursors.

Working first on the pair of tables nearest the circulation desk, Jack was tricked. He thought, *This is going to be a breeze.* There were only six or seven wads of gum per table, and most of them were not sticky at all. He didn't even have to tip the tables on their sides, but was simply able to lean over and reach up with the putty knife. He only had to use the OFFIT two or three times.

But as Jack worked his way toward the back of the deep room the volume of gum increased. Dramatically.

Distance from the librarian = safer chewing = more gum.

By the time he reached the seventh and eighth tables, Jack was digging and chipping his way through gum that was sometimes more than half an inch thick. He felt like an archaeologist performing an excavation, examining clues left by a vanished civilization—Minnesota Jack and the Temple of Goo.

He began to count gum layers, like counting growth rings on a tree stump. He noticed the subtle difference in color between peppermint and spearmint gum, the sharp contrast in scent and texture between chewing gum and bubble gum.

Examining the deposits from recent years, Jack found an extraordinary range of colors. There were blues of every shade and at least fifteen different pinks. There were deep reds, bright turquoises, and soft aquamarines. Brilliant oranges, glaring yellows, and muted greens of a dozen different hues rounded out the spectrum.

Occasionally a group of gum wads would suggest an image to Jack's wandering mind, like cloud formations on a summer afternoon. He saw a shape that reminded him of his grandfather's face. He saw cars and houses, birds, and an elephant.

Mrs. Stokely interrupted. She had her coat and hat on. Looking into the bucket where Jack had been dropping the scrapings, she said, "My goodness, I had no idea there could be that much gum in here, and you're only a little more than half done!" Jack groaned inwardly at that. "Well, good night, and be sure to pull the door shut when you go, Jack."

Jack looked up at the clock. He had another fifteen minutes.

Back on task and thinking scientifically now,

Jack noticed how the gum formed two crude, over-lapping semicircles on the bottom of the table above each chair. Four chairs, eight semicircles. Simple—one semicircle for the right-handed gum stickers, the other for lefties.

The radius of each semicircle was about the length of a kid's arm from the elbow to the finger-tips. He observed that, overall, kids using fingers to jam gum onto the table outnumbered those using thumbs. Jack also noticed that kids using their left hand to off-load gum were twice as likely to use their thumb as the kids using their right hand.

The fluorescent lights were not quite bright enough to create clear contrast, but on some of the wads he could see perfect fingerprints pressed into the gum. Jack thought, *I wonder if Ackerby knows about this.*

By the end of his hour in the library Jack was ready to give a long and scholarly lecture:

*"A Very Sticky Decade"*
*by Professor Jack Rankin*
*Chairman, Department of Chewology*

Hurrying back to the empty shop, Jack put his stuff away in the supply closet. Then he had a thought.

He got another plastic bucket from the stack and knocked the day's gum scrapings into it. He estimated that it was about a half gallon of chewed gum of every color imaginable. Grinning, he set the bucket in the corner. Maybe a gallon or two of dead gum could be used for something. At the very least, it was . . . interesting—in a creepy, disgusting sort of way.

Then Jack moved fast, hoping to be gone before anyone came. He pulled a piece of paper out of his backpack and wrote a hurried note.

*Dear Dad—*
   *I didn't take the bus, so can I ride home with you? I'm going to find a quiet place and do homework. I'll meet you back here at five, OK?*
                                                                 *Jack*

He left the note on his dad's desk, weighed it down with a stapler, and turned on the lamp. His dad would be sure to see it.

Then he grabbed his coat and backpack and headed for the stairs. He had almost an hour and a half.

The tower was waiting.

## Chapter 13

# ALtituDe

An empty school can be spooky. In a building that's seventy-five years old it's a feeling that's hard to shake.

Jack walked quietly up the east stairwell, every sense on alert. At the second-floor landing he stopped. He could hear Arnie shaking his dust mop just around the corner. Jack waited, holding his breath. When the heavy footsteps headed away, he rounded the corner and kept climbing.

The thick slate treads on the stairs were worn smooth from countless thousands of trudging feet, but Jack's shoes barely touched down as he headed up and up.

The fourth floor was the end of the line. It was also where his dad had been fixing a toilet, and maybe he still was.

Jack had been up on four only once or twice, and not at all this year. All of the fifth-grade classrooms were on the second floor, except for gym and music.

The tower rose from the middle of the building, so Jack went to his right. He edged his way down the corridor. He passed a hallway that ran south toward the back of the school.

He reached the exact center of the building, just where he thought there would have to be a door, but there was nothing. Frustrated, Jack stopped to think.

Then it dawned on him. The door to the tower could be along either of the two hallways that ran back from the long front corridor. The question was, if his dad was still working up here, which of the two north-south halls was he in? A loud *clank* from his right answered that question. Jack headed back the way he had come, and when he got to the hallway he'd passed a minute before, turned right.

There were classrooms and lockers on the left side of the hall. Jack was focused on the right. Lockers, three classrooms, a girls bathroom, and then . . . a door.

There was no number on the door, no lettering.

Digging into his front pocket, Jack pulled out a key.

Number 73. Wrong one.

Digging again, he pulled out key 501 and slid it into the lock. Holding his breath, he applied pressure and the key turned.

He was in.

The hinges creaked and Jack stopped. He tried inching the door open, but that made the creaking worse. Hoping that the distance would hide the sound from his dad, he gave the door a bold shove, got himself inside, pulled the key out of the lock, and shut the door behind him, holding the knob so the latch wouldn't click.

Darkness.

It smelled musty, closed in.

He groped around on the wall and found a light switch. He flipped it, and instead of bright fluorescence there was the shadowy glow of a single bare bulb.

He was in a narrow passage, made narrower by things piled along the right-hand wall. Stacks of old books. A heap of broken chairs. A discolored state flag in an iron floor stand. There was a pile of torn roller maps and five or six dusty globes. Bookcases with jumbled shelves were stacked three high.

It was an educational graveyard.

Jack picked his way, careful not to let his backpack bump anything. Just past the bookcases there was another door. Its doorknob had no place for a key.

With his heart racing, Jack turned the knob and pushed. Pale daylight filtered down from above, and ten feet in front of him lay the first flight of tower stairs. Walking in and peering up, he saw that there were five more flights, maybe six.

At the first landing there was a narrow window, but the glass was so grimy Jack could hardly see through it. The window at the second landing was even worse.

But at the third landing Jack sucked in a quick breath. This window was on the front of the tower, the side facing north toward the front lawn. The window was much cleaner, and a partial view of Huntington lay spread out before him.

Someone had hauled one of the old wooden chairs up to the landing. Its broken rungs had been artfully spliced and then held in place with a few turns of twisted wire. Jack dragged the chair over to the window and stood on the seat to get a clearer view from the top panes.

Craning his neck to look northwest, he could see where Randall Street crossed the railroad tracks. He counted six blocks north of the tracks—that was his street, Greenwood. The leafless trees didn't hide much, and by counting off the brick bungalows from the corner, he thought he could see the roof of his own home.

The bright October air was frosty and clear, and the flat land of the upper Midwest stretched on and on, dotted here and there with ponds and lakes.

Northward on the distant horizon he thought he could see Minneapolis, just the hint of a skyline.

Jack kept going up. The fourth and fifth landings each had windows, but Jack wanted to get to the top. He wanted to reach the summit.

At the sixth landing Jack had to crouch. The concrete ceiling above it was only about four feet tall. And there was a metal hatch.

He shrugged off his backpack and set it on the floor. Then Jack reached up, turned the handle on the hatch, put his shoulder against the steel, and straightened up.

Forty or fifty pigeons took flight with such a sudden noise that Jack dropped back into the opening, terrified. Then, realizing what had made the sound, he quickly stood up again, his head and shoulders above the level of the bell platform.

The fresh air was chilly, and the brightness made his eyes smart. He reached down for his backpack and swung it up, then pulled himself onto the platform. It was a square about twelve feet wide. Each side had two arches with a round limestone pillar that went to the floor between them. Chicken wire had been fastened across all the openings to keep the pigeons out, and for the most part, it had worked.

In the middle of the space a pair of I beams about six feet tall were set into the concrete floor, and a third one was bolted between them. Three bronze bells hung from the cross beam. Each bell had a clapper in the center, along with some kind of black metal box that almost touched the outer rim, probably some kind of electric bell ringer.

The largest bell was about two feet across, and the smallest was only about a foot. Jack had the urge to grab the clapper of the biggest bell and start swinging. He resisted.

Jack kept low to the floor under the bells in the center, partly to keep from being seen by anyone who might glance up, but mostly to keep from feeling like he was going to plunge to his death. The view was dizzying, spectacular, a true panorama. Westward toward the town center he could see the green copper roof of the public library, and a little farther on, the gold eagle on the town hall weather vane, up above the treetops.

Turning in a slow circle, Jack picked out all the places he knew. It was like looking at a picture book of his life. The park near his house, the one with the tall swing set. His elementary school. The Good Shepherd Lutheran Church. Grampa Parkman's house. Capitol Bank, where he had his savings account—almost three hundred dollars. Half a mile to the south he could see the metal framing and some brick walls of the new junior high. And off to the west the red roof of the gymnasium at the new high school caught the afternoon sun.

It was all there—his past, his present, his future.

And that made Jack feel good.

Until he saw Grampa's house again. Then he thought, *Mom has lived here all her life—and so has Dad. It's his town too. He grew up here. What if I'm growing up to be just like him?*

Out loud Jack said, "But I am *not* like him!" The fierceness in his own voice startled him, and another cloud of pigeons took off from the roof of the tower.

Grabbing a pen, he flipped his notebook open to a blank page and wrote at the top,

> Ways I Am NOT Like My Dad
>
> I like to keep <u>my</u> room messy.
> I am not going to live in Huntington
> when I grow up.
> I do <u>not</u> like to clean things.
> I read more books.
> I am going to go to college.
> I am great at using computers.
> I like loud music.

The list filled most of the page, and toward the end Jack even wrote, "I hate tomatoes."

Scanning the list made Jack feel better, and when he glanced down at the town, Huntington looked good again, safer. Jack closed his binder and then got out his math book, a spiral notebook, and a pencil. He zipped his jacket and pulled up the hood. He leaned against one of the bell supports and angled himself to catch the best light.

He'd found a quiet place, and now he was doing his homework, just like he'd said in the note to his dad.

Math went fast—it was always easy for Jack. Then he opened up the book he was reading in English, *The Indian in the Cupboard*. He had read it before, but that didn't matter. He always read the books he liked again and again. He was supposed to stop after chapter four, but the action swept him along. He knew exactly how Omri felt, and Little Bear, too.

Looking up some time later, Jack saw it was getting dark. He shivered, and his back ached from leaning against the steel post. He hadn't noticed while he was reading.

Leaning forward near the pillar at the front of the tower, Jack could just read the time and temperature sign at his bank down on Main Street.

Four fifty-three. Only seven minutes to get back to the shop in time to meet his dad. Jack said he'd be there at five, and he would be. He hadn't been late for anything in years—not school, not a rehearsal, not a single assignment.

It was downhill all the way to the shop, and Jack made it with a minute to spare.

Chapter 14

# HomeWARD

John Rankin's Chevy pickup was getting to be an antique. It was a '72, but if it hadn't been for the changes in styling, no one would have guessed. The original green paint was still in great shape, and underneath the denim seat covers the vinyl seats weren't worn at all.

The old green Chevy didn't look like some trophy truck, the kind you see at a truck rally at the Holiday Inn on a Sunday afternoon. This was a real truck, a working truck. It was a tool, and John Rankin took good care of his tools.

Climbing up onto the seat next to his dad, Jack knew the routine by heart. Pump the gas pedal four times. Pull the choke lever out two clicks. Count to fifteen, turn the key, and *vooOOOm*, the engine jumps to life. Worked every time, heart of summer or dead of winter.

Jack was glad it was so late, and almost dark, too. He didn't want any kids to see him riding with his dad. Jack thought, *And that's another thing that's different. I'd never want a truck, and my dad has had this one forever.*

Easing out of the back lot onto Summer Street, his dad asked, "So how was the library?"

Jack said, "Not so bad."

"Hmmm."

They waited for the light to change, and John Rankin sat stiffly, both hands on the steering wheel, his index fingers tapping along with the clicking turn signal.

Jack wanted to know what his dad thought about him messing up that desk—and why he hadn't even yelled at him. Now would be the perfect time to talk . . . maybe even say he was sorry.

The light seemed to stay red forever. The silence felt uncomfortable, but Jack couldn't think of what to say. Then he remembered his talk with the librarian. "Mrs. Stokely said it was hard to get the library moved last summer." His voice sounded too loud.

His dad nodded and said, "Yup." He put the truck into first gear and pulled forward.

Jack saw they weren't heading toward home. Instead of turning north onto Randall Street, they kept going west on Main Street and turned onto South Grand Boulevard. Jack pictured where they were, remembering how the town had looked from the top of the tower.

Waiting at the next traffic light, John Rankin cleared his throat. Trying to sound casual, he said, "You get teased much about your dad being a janitor?"

The question caught Jack by surprise, but he didn't show it. "Nah. One or two kids have said stuff, but they're jerks. I don't pay any attention to it."

"That's good. Hate to think you're getting razzed on my account." His dad fell silent again.

Jack could have opened up and said a lot more, but he stopped himself. Thinking about having a talk was easier than actually doing it.

The light changed, and the traffic eased ahead. Jack looked out at the store windows and the new-car dealerships, and his dad kept focused on his driving. It was rush hour in Huntington. There were no real slowdowns, but the major streets were pretty full for twenty or thirty minutes every afternoon.

After a mile or so, his dad pulled the truck up next to the curb in front of a big used-car lot and shut off the engine. "I know I've told you that my dad was in the car business." Pointing to the right, out the window by Jack, he said, "My dad used to own that lot back in the fifties—Honest Phil Rankin. He ran it right up to the day he died. That man could sell anything to anybody, and he made a good bit of money—it's his money that's going to put you and your sister through college before too long."

He paused, both hands back on the steering wheel.

Jack looked over at his dad's face, lit up by the string of bulbs that ran above the first row of cars. His eyes were open, but he wasn't really looking at anything.

"I worked for my dad every Saturday morning from the time I was twelve until I left home to join the army. Hated it. I washed cars, all year-round, every Saturday, sometimes after school, too. Hardly got paid at all.

"He used to bring a customer over to where I was washing. He'd come near on purpose and do his sales pitch, and when the deal was closed, he'd come find me. He waves a check or a stack of fifty-dollar bills at me. 'Did you hear how I did that?' he says. 'See how I cut off every possible escape? I hope you listen good, Johnny boy, because some-day this is going to be your place. You learn how to do this right, and it's like finding money on the sidewalk.' I nodded and just kept on washing. I didn't like to think about that."

John Rankin paused, reaching for words. Jack could tell he was forcing himself to talk. His dad had never said this much to him at one time before, not even when they used to go fishing and sit together all day in the old red canoe.

"And you know what really drove me crazy?"

Jack shook his head but immediately felt silly. His dad wasn't waiting for a response from him. He was years and years away.

"I never had a car—no car, all during high school. Here it would have been so easy for my dad to set me up with any old car, just something to call my own, just a little independence. But that wasn't his way.

"Then one Saturday night when I was a senior in high school, I swiped his office keys, went down to the lot, and drove off in a red Corvette. I was borrowing it, just for the night."

Jack hardly breathed. Almost without meaning to, he slipped a hand into his right pocket and felt the two keys he had "borrowed."

As he described the Corvette, a little smile played at the corners of his dad's mouth. "That was quite a rig, let me tell you. First gear would run out to fifty miles an hour. Way too much car for me. And wouldn't you know, I whacked that thing into a phone pole about a mile and a half from here. That fiberglass body just broke up into a million pieces."

Jack gasped. "You mean you *totaled* a Corvette? Did you get hurt?"

"I was shaken up, and I had a cut on my chin, but I was mostly okay. The car was another story. That thing wasn't even good for parts. Bent the frame, cracked the engine block. Blue-book price was sixty-five hundred dollars—that's still a lot of money, but back then that was a *whole* lot of money."

Jack asked, "What did your dad say?"

"He came right over to the hospital, of course, but he didn't even ask if I was all right. First thing he says is, 'You got a big debt to pay off, mister. And you're going to pay it too. This summer you're coming to work for me—full-time. You got college plans, but till you dig out of this hole, you can forget all about 'em.'

"Well, I was never going to be some used-car salesman, not even for a summer. And I told him so. 'You're just a loud-mouthed junk dealer in a cheap sport coat.' That's what I said to him. And I said I'd rather join the army than work for him. And come next morning that's what I did, just to spite him. And I don't know what hurt him worse—calling him a junk dealer or me running off to the army."

The flow of the story seemed to stop, but Jack felt there was more coming. He waited, and his dad began speaking again, his voice a little quieter.

"You were about two years old when your grandpa died. At the wake a man came up to me and said, 'Your daddy gave me a car one afternoon, and he made me promise I'd never tell a soul. That car got me to and from my first job for three years. Your dad was quite a guy.' I thought the man was nuts. He had to be thinking of someone else.

"But then the next day at the funeral three other people came up and said almost the same thing.

"Well, your mom and me, we went through all my dad's papers, and sure enough, every year he gave away one or two cars—about thirty in all over the years. That's a lot of money. I mean, these weren't fancy cars, and old Honest Phil figured out how to take some tax deductions, but still. And we found a box of letters from the people he'd helped out. It was like a whole part of himself he never let me see. And I thought, 'If he could give all these cars away to strangers, why couldn't he give just one to me?' Took me a long time to figure that one out."

Jack asked, "Was he just being stingy?"

John Rankin shook his head. "If he was stingy, then he wouldn't have given all those cars away. No, I think he just wanted me to learn that I had to make my own way. He loved me, and he didn't want me to be spoiled."

Jack had been watching his dad's face as he told the story. He had that same feeling he got from one of those trick puzzles—the kind where you stare and stare, and a picture suddenly appears. He was just beginning to see a new image.

Jack and his dad sat quietly. The traffic kept whizzing by, and two or three couples were walking around the lot, looking at the used cars. The salespeople circled like eagles.

Then the traffic slowed to a crawl, and a guy driving a big blue Oldsmobile leaned on his horn right next to the pickup. Both Jack and John jumped in their seats, and then laughed nervously.

John put the truck in neutral and reached for the ignition. As he started the engine he turned to look at Jack. "Just so you know it for good and sure, I don't expect you'll ever be a janitor, Jackie. My life is my life, and yours is yours. I'm just glad that we get to run side by side for a few years, that's all."

Checking the rearview mirror, he said, "Now,

we'd better shoot on home, or your mom'll start calling the hospitals."

The green pickup bucked a little in first gear as John Rankin edged out into the stream of traffic on South Grand Boulevard.

At the next corner he swung a right turn onto Oak Street and headed north.

During that short drive home Jack realized two things.

He didn't know much about his dad—hardly anything.

And he definitely wanted to know more.

Chapter 15

# DISCOVERIES

As he hauled his gum-busting equipment around the high school, it began to dawn on Jack just how huge the place was. It was like four of his old elementary schools stacked up, one on top of the other. Four times more floor space, four times as many classrooms and wastebaskets and pencil sharpeners, four times as many lights and light switches and radiators, four times as many restrooms and sinks, not to mention the gyms and the locker rooms and the industrial arts shops and all the rest of it.

And it all worked. It was more than seventy-five years old, and everything worked every day. Jack tried to imagine what it would be like to be responsible for keeping the whole place going, and quickly gave up. It was almost too much to think about.

It took Jack two more scraping sessions to get the library free of gum.

The last four tables were the worst, and by the time he was done with all the chairs, the three-gallon bucket tucked behind the door in the supply closet was nearly full of gum. The loaded bucket weighed about twenty pounds, and it gave off a sickening combination of odd, gummy smells. Jack kept his gum bucket covered with a cloth to keep the odor from filling the supply closet.

Looking at his pail of trophies, Jack thought, *I wonder if I've invented a new category for* The Guinness Book of World Records?—*Greatest Quantity of Gum Ever Removed from School Property during Four Hours!*

Both Wednesday and Thursday Jack had wanted to stay late like he had on Tuesday. He discovered he was actually looking forward to another ride home with his dad. It seemed like there was never time to talk to him at home. Dad was always tired, or spending time with Mom—and then there was Lois, the world's biggest pest. Another ride home would be good.

Jack thought a lot about what his dad had told him on Tuesday, and now he wanted to ask him a million questions. Especially about the Vietnam War, about being in the army. Jack also wanted to know more about his grandfather, Honest Phil. And about how Dad and Mom met and got married. Tons of questions.

Jack had also wanted to stay late so he could use the time after gum patrol to search for the door that matched key number 73. He'd been on the lookout. He watched for doors in odd places, but Jack was pretty sure he would not find the steam tunnel door without a serious hunting expedition.

Still, as much as he wanted to stay, on Wednesday and Thursday he went right home because he had too much work. He had to do a big social studies project about the thirteen original colonies, and he had to prepare an oral report on *The Indian in the Cupboard.* The project and the book report were both due on Monday—another conspiracy hatched by evil teachers to overwork him.

Jack sometimes wished he could put things off to the last minute, but he just wasn't glued together that way. He had to start an assignment the moment it was given and work steadily until it was out of the way. It was like he couldn't help it. He had to get things done on time, had to be places on time.

So Jack had ridden the late bus home on both Wednesday and Thursday, right after gum patrol.

Friday morning there was a light dusting of snow over Huntington. Jack listened to the morning newscast, and a woman reported that there had been a full three inches in Minneapolis overnight, and that it looked like it was going to be a snowy fall and winter. As if that were news in Minnesota.

Jack loved snow, and the more the better.

But, walking into the old high school, Jack noticed what the snow and salt and sand were doing to the floors.

Instantly Jack thought of his dad.

He realized that his dad probably hated to see the first snow. The long, cold Minnesota winter must mean a lot of extra work for him.

Mrs. Lambert wasn't in the room when the bell rang at the start of Friday's math class, and Jack wished she were. Kirk Dorfmann had not taken any more cheap shots at him, but that was just because he hadn't had the opportunity. In the halls Kirk and Luke laid off because they were afraid of what Pete might do. Math class was the only other time Jack saw them, and Mrs. Lambert had kept a sharp lookout for trouble.

Kirk had been moved two rows away from Jack, and the distance helped. The problem was that Luke Karnes sat between them.

Making sure that Kirk was watching, Luke pulled a piece of pink gum out of his mouth and made a big show of sticking it to the underside of his desk. Then he said, "Hey, Kirk, do you think I should get old John to clean this off? . . . Or should we ask Ackerby to have young Jackie do it?"

Kirk gave a little sneer and said, "What's the difference? If you've seen one janitor, you've seen 'em all."

Jack ignored both of them. They were idiots, completely clueless—pathetic. Jack found it remarkable, but he wasn't even tempted to trade words with them, much less trade punches. It was like he had moved into a whole different world, and they were still stuck somewhere else, trying to reach him.

But Luke wasn't done. He felt like he needed to impress Kirk today, and he thought Jack was ignoring him out of fear.

Big mistake.

Luke reached across the aisle and flicked Jack's ear. "What's the matter, Jackie? Didn't your hear me, or are you just acting *stuck up*?"

Jack didn't lose his temper, but he did respond. Glancing quickly back toward the door to be sure Mrs. Lambert was still absent, he swung left to face Luke, his legs out in the aisle. Before Luke could even flinch, Jack stuck his right foot under Luke's long leg, just behind the knee, and lifted the leg straight up—no violence, just a little muscle.

Luke pulled his leg away, and Jack didn't try to

stop him. Jack had accomplished his mission. Because as Luke jerked his leg away he banged it against the bottom of his desk and jammed it right into his own gob of fresh, sticky gum.

As Jack swung around to face front again Mrs. Lambert walked in the classroom door. Striding to the front of the room, she said, "Quiet down, everyone. I know how you all hate to miss even a little bit of your precious math class, so please get your homework out."

Then Mrs. Lambert noticed Luke trying to deal with the pink blob that was smeared onto the right leg of his new Abercrombie corduroys. Turning around, she pulled a tissue from the box on her desk. "Here, Luke, just cover it up for now so it doesn't get stuck anywhere else. I've told you never to bring gum into my classroom, haven't I? *That* is one of the reasons why."

With a perfectly straight face Jack said, "Hey, Luke, there's this stuff that'll take that mess right out. Stop down in the janitor's shop sometime, and I'll show you what to do."

Mrs. Lambert smiled and said, "That's nice of you, Jack."

And Jack said, "Oh, it's nothing—all in a day's work."

## Chapter 16

# Behind the Curtain

After school Jack was surprised to find Mr. Ackerby waiting for him in the workshop. His first thought was that Luke Karnes had ratted, and now he would have a whole bunch of new trouble.

Mr. Ackerby said, "Hello, Jack. I wanted you to know that I've been checking up on you. I got a good report from Mrs. Stokely. She says you're a hard worker, and I'm glad to hear it."

Jack nodded and tried to look pleasant. Mr. Ackerby's compliment was sort of like having the jailer praise you for being a wonderful little prisoner.

Mr. Ackerby went on. "I also came down here to find John. I feel pretty stupid not realizing right away that you were his son. I worked with him on our move all summer long. We'd come up against a problem, and he'd figure out a way to solve it, every time. He certainly has this building in great shape. A big place this old doesn't keep working all by itself, that's for sure."

Jack didn't know what to say, so he just nodded and said, "Yeah."

Mr. Ackerby was used to having kids feel uncomfortable when he talked to them—it was usually what he wanted. But he'd snooped around, and he had learned that Jack Rankin was a pretty good kid. Good student, honest, and rarely in trouble. Every teacher Mr. Ackerby had approached seemed quite surprised about the incident in music class.

So Mr. Ackerby was trying to give their relationship a friendlier tone. He asked, "Where are you working today?"

Jack said, "I have to start in the auditorium," and to himself Jack added, —*thanks to you and your slave labor program.*

Mr. Ackerby nodded, his eyebrows lifting. "Another big job. Well, I won't keep you. I'm going to wait here another few minutes to see if I can catch your dad. And, Jack . . . what with the three-day weekend coming up and all, if you want to cut out at three today instead of three thirty, that'll be okay."

"Um . . . yeah. Thanks." Pretty chintzy gift, but it was better than nothing.

Jack left the workshop with a new impression of Mr. Ackerby.

The guy seemed almost human.

Mr. Ackerby was the second person who had said that cleaning gum in the auditorium would be a big job. When Jack told Lou where he would be working, Lou whistled and then said, "Well, nobody's going to accuse your daddy of giving you special treatment, that's for sure."

So it would be a big job. So what? The bigger the better. He was Jack, the Fearless One, the Climber of Towers, the Keeper of the Keys.

Ready to do battle, Jack pulled open the center door at the back of the auditorium.

His heart sank.

He stood there, one medium-size boy armed with a red bucket and a putty knife.

Eight hundred seventy-five folding seats stared at him in silent defiance.

The place was vast. The floor sloped sharply downward toward a wide stage. The dusty gold curtain was two-thirds open, and the area back-stage was completely dark.

The pale green walls needed fresh paint. High windows along the east wall let in the gloomy afternoon light. It looked to Jack like more snow was on the way.

The theater-style seats swung in a graceful arc,

with an aisle on the east and west, and one up the center. The backs and seat bottoms were covered with fake brown leather fastened on by brass upholstery tacks. And the wooden underside of almost every seat was pockmarked with wads of gum.

With a deep sigh Jack set down his bucket and began removing gum from the bottom of seat number 1 in row W. The scraping and rubbing sounds that had seemed so loud in the library were lost in the huge room, as if they floated off into outer space.

Jack got into the rhythm of the work. Seat by seat he moved across the wide back row, turned the corner, and headed back. He would work on a seat until it was done, straighten up, push the bucket forward with his foot, then bend down and start the next one. He scraped carefully, trying not to scratch the dark plywood, and he wasn't satisfied until a seat bottom was completely clean.

By the time he had cleaned two rows, it was getting so dark that sometimes Jack couldn't tell if he had got all the gum off by scraping, or if he should use the OFFIT to finish the job. He put his putty knife in the bucket, went to the center aisle, and walked downhill toward the stage. Time to turn on some lights.

Vaulting easily up onto the front of the stage, Jack walked behind the curtain toward the right, his footsteps hollow on the wooden floor. He had worked on the lighting crew for a play at his old school, and he knew what to look for. Somewhere there had to be a switch labeled HOUSE LIGHTS. He headed for the right-hand wall.

Backstage was a mess. Music stands and folding chairs were scattered about, and a set of dented kettledrums was half covered by large cardboard panels. They were pieces of scenery that had been painted to look like big blocks of stone along the top of a castle wall. A rack that used to hold costumes had tipped over, and wire coat hangers lay in a tangled heap.

Jack's eyes adjusted to the darkness of the stage, and he could see there was no light panel near the right-hand door. He did an about-face and headed left, walking along the back wall of the stage area.

Near the middle of the stage Jack tripped on something and went sprawling onto the floor. Rubbing his elbow, he stood up and looked back to see what had caused the fall. It was the silver blade of a long sword, half hidden by a black curtain covering the rear wall of the stage. He bent over, pulled the whole thing out from behind the curtain, and straightened up to get a good look at it.

It was just a stage prop, made of wood. But it had been well made and carefully painted. It was a knight's broadsword, with a wide hilt and a long handle, made to be swung using both hands. It was almost four feet long.

Jack swung it, and it made a pleasant whirring sound as he carved the air. It felt good in his hands. Holding it out in front of him at eye level, he lunged toward the curtain, pretending to jab the Evil Knight.

A *clank* came from behind the curtain—maybe armor or something. There was a break in the curtain about six feet to his left, so Jack walked over, grabbed it, and held on as he stepped about ten paces back toward the right.

Just as Jack suspected, more stuff lay hidden behind the curtain. He saw a long jousting lance made from a bamboo pole, and a shield that had once been a metal trash can lid. It had been spray-painted white and then decorated with a red lion wearing a gold crown.

But that wasn't the best thing. The best thing had nothing to do with knights and armor and swordplay. The best thing was very simple.

It was a door.

On the door there was just one word.

ACCESS.

Jack put down his wooden sword and reached into his pocket. He pulled out a key. The light was too dim to see the number, but he could feel there were only two numerals stamped on it. It had to be key 73.

He pushed the key into the jagged keyhole, held his breath, and turned.

Bingo.

The door hinged on the left, and Jack pulled it open wide. Peering into the shadows, he saw a short landing just inside the door, and a set of metal stairs—nine steps down, maybe more. It was very dark in there.

There was a light switch on the wall to the right of the landing, but when Jack flipped it, nothing happened.

Suddenly aware of how his heart was pounding, Jack let himself off the hook. There was no hurry.

Now that the door was found, he could take his time, gather some equipment, do a proper exploration. No need to go rushing down into . . . into that place.

So he started to shut the door.

And when he had the door almost shut, Jack noticed something strange.

When a door is almost shut, there's usually a flow of air—either in or out. The flow of air hitting Jack in the face was coming out of the tunnel.

Nothing strange about that.

It wasn't the air itself that was odd. It was what the air was carrying.

The air was carrying a smell.

It was faint, so faint that Jack thought he must be imagining it—but it was a smell Jack knew very well. . . . Too well.

It was the smell of watermelon bubble gum.

## Chapter 17

# One-Way Ticket

Jack sniffed the air coming out of the steam tunnel again, carefully. Nothing now. But there really had been the barest hint before, in that first rush of upward air. Watermelon bubble gum. Jack was sure. Well, he was pretty sure.

Gently, Jack closed the door. He pulled the black curtain to cover it again, tucking the wooden sword out of sight.

Abandoning his search for the auditorium lights, he hurried across the stage, jumped down to the floor, and trotted up to where he had left his bucket. Jack looked up at the clock and saw it was already three forty-five. He had missed out on Mr. Ackerby's offer to quit early. Maybe the offer would carry over to Tuesday?

He ran silently through the halls. When he reached the door at the top of the workshop stairs, Jack paused to listen. If possible, he wanted to get in, borrow a few important items, and then get back to the auditorium without meeting anyone.

He didn't hear anything, so he opened the door and scooted down the stairs. He put his supplies away and then went over to his dad's desk. He was betting there would be a flashlight in it somewhere, and he was right. In the top right drawer there was a small black Mag-Lite with the name of a plumbing supply company printed on its side in gold letters. Jack twisted the end and the light came on, bright and steady. Perfect.

He tucked the light in his back pocket and went over to the workbench, trying to imagine what else he might need. He couldn't really think of anything else, not for a quick first look. But when he saw a spool of nylon string, his mind flashed to the story in *Huckleberry Finn,* the part where Huck and Tom get lost in the caves. Jack grabbed the spool and stuffed it into the outer pocket of his backpack. Then he pulled out his old white Minnesota Vikings cap and put it on.

He was all set to leave, was actually on the stairs, and then stopped. He needed to leave a note for his dad. It was Friday, and Jack was sure his dad would want to leave right at five.

Rushing back to the desk, he scribbled the message and dashed back up to the landing, where he almost collided with Lou.

Lou flattened up against the wall, exaggerating his close call. "Whoa, there. Where you off to in such a big hurry? Late bus already left. You about ran me down."

Jack said, "Sorry, Lou. I'm going to go and study for a while, maybe walk over to the library or something. Then I'm going to ride home with my dad. I left him a note."

Lou hurried down the stairs and grabbed the gray toolbox off the cluttered bench. "Your dad sent me to get the toolbox, and he said if you were still here, would you mind cleaning up the bench for him while you're waiting? We've got a busted door he wants to get fixed before quittin' time." Lou was already back at the landing. "So I'll just tell him I gave you the message, okay? If I don't see you again, you have a good weekend, Jackie."

Jack stood on the landing. Looking down, he could see that the workbench was a wreck after a busy week. He used to love putting it all back in order when he came to visit his dad at work. *Yeah,* Jack thought, *back when I was about six. First I've got to scrape junk off of ten thousand seats, and then I have to clean up his messes, too? No way.*

Jack stomped back down the steps, crumpled the first note he'd left, and tossed it into the trash. On a new piece of paper he scrawled,

*Dad—*

*Couldn't clean up the bench.*
*I have some other stuff I've got to do.*
*See you at five.*

*Jack*


Jack made sure that no one saw him go back into the auditorium.

Walking directly to the back of the stage, he left the wall curtain in place. No sense advertising that someone was here. He took out the spool of string, set his backpack and jacket on the floor beside the door, and turned on the flashlight. Pulling both keys from his pocket, he chose the right one and opened the door, just a crack.

He wanted to check himself. Had he just imagined that watermelon smell?

Jack sniffed the airflow. He shook his head and sniffed again.

Nothing, at least nothing he could recognize. Mostly it smelled like his basement at home, but not as damp.

Stepping inside the doorway onto the metal landing, Jack shone the light down the steps. Five steps ran down to a short corridor maybe fifteen feet long and only about three feet wide. The floor of the corridor was concrete, and the walls were terra-cotta building bricks, the hollow kind. The ceiling was also concrete, a little less than six feet high. At the end of the corridor there was an opening, no door, just an opening, rectangular and dark.

Jack wanted to leave the access door open, but it swung outward too far on its own. He tried putting his backpack against it, but then his backpack made a bulge in the velvet curtain that hid the door. Shining the flashlight around to see if there was something else to prop it with, he saw the wooden sword. He bent down and picked it up. Smiling, he decided to take it with him. After all, most of the really great explorers had swords, didn't they?

Sword in hand, he stepped back inside onto the landing and bravely pulled the door shut behind him.

Instantly he wished he hadn't, and he reached for the knob on the inside of the door. It wouldn't turn. Shining the light, Jack saw why. It was a double-keyed door. It needed a key to open it from the inside, too.

Reaching into his pocket, Jack froze. He only had one key. He didn't even bother getting it out to shine the light on it. He knew it was the wrong one, the tower key.

He needed the other key.

It was close, only about six inches away.

But Jack couldn't reach it.

Key number 73 was sticking from the lock on the outside of the door.

## Chapter 18

# UNDERGROUND

Jack had known panic before.

When he was four, he had wandered away from his mom at a big department store in Minneapolis, lost for half an hour.

That was panic.

There was the time just last summer in the deep end of the municipal swimming pool. He had come up for a big gulp of air and got water instead.

That was panic too.

But this, this was different.

It was as if Jack had discovered a new land.

Off in the distance there were sheer mountains of panic poking into a dark and twisted sky. Frantic waterfalls and desperate rivers of liquid panic swept toward him with a churning noise that blotted out all thought. Standing there on the landing, flashlight in one hand, wooden sword in the other, Jack saw before him an entire unexplored continent of pure, numbing terror.

His heart pounded.

His hands shook.

And his mind raced.

It was Friday afternoon before a three-day weekend.

The school was emptying fast.

He was trapped.

He was cold.

And no one knew where he was. But Jack could change that. He could kick on the door. He could scream and pound and yell for help.

And Jack did, for two full minutes.

Then he stopped, his ears ringing, his hands hurting, breathing hard.

And he listened. Nothing.

The sound had been muffled by soft velvet curtains. And the little noise that made it across the stage had been swallowed whole by the yawning auditorium.

Jack felt completely alone—but only for about twenty seconds.

Small scritching sounds came from the darkness behind him.

Wheeling around, the beam of his flashlight caught the flick of a long pink tail as it disappeared through the low doorway.

Rats.

An involuntary shiver shook him. All of a sudden the wooden sword Jack gripped in his hand didn't seem silly at all.

Did the beam of light flicker? Hard to say how long the flashlight had been lying in his dad's desk. Batteries don't last forever.

Then Jack remembered.

Maybe there was someone else in the tunnels, someone other than him and the rats. Someone who liked watermelon gum.

And that someone must know how to get in and out.

Maybe there would even be a way to get out without being caught, without having to deal with Mr. Ackerby again.

Jack's Vikings cap had fallen off while he was pounding on the door. He picked it up, put it on. Then he walked down the steps, along the short corridor, and ducked through the opening into the main tunnel.

The tunnel was about five feet wide, its ceiling as high as the one in the access corridor. It ran off in both directions farther than his light would shine. A large pipe ran along the roof near the right-hand wall, suspended by steel rods embedded in the ceiling. It looked like cantaloupes could have rolled through the iron cylinder with ease.

Every twenty feet or so there was a joint, like a round steel collar, studded with six large nuts and bolts.

An electrical line ran along the center of the ceiling, with lightbulb sockets at intervals. Some were broken, some were missing, but others looked fine. Scanning the area, Jack saw no switch.

There were some other bundles of wire running the length of the tunnel on the side opposite the pipeline. Some looked like electrical wires, some looked like telephone cables.

The floor of the tunnel was level and smooth, and to Jack's relief there were no rats in sight. An old paper cup and a dusty soda can lay on the floor near the opening, evidence of some workman's lunch or coffee break. A thick layer of dust coated the floor. There were footprints—rats' and humans'. But with no weather to disturb them, the human footprints could have been decades old.

Decision time: Walk right or left?

Jack sniffed, and smelled nothing. There was no airflow, which made sense—no open door. Then he crouched down and leaned over so his nose was only about six inches from the floor. The air was cooler close to the floor, and there seemed to be a flow coming from the right.

Jack's instinct was to walk toward where the air was coming from. But what if there were a lot of little flows? So Jack ran a test.

Turning to his left, Jack walked fifty paces, stopped, stooped, and got his face down near the floor again. The flow of air was weaker, but it was still coming from the same direction. Turning back to his right, he walked the fifty paces back to the access opening. By going to the right, Jack was pretty sure he would be walking in a westerly direction, basically parallel with Main Street, headed toward the public library, the police station, and downtown Huntington. At least that's the way it seemed. Jack decided to go right.

With a direction established, Jack did not hesitate. He walked.

As he walked Jack's mind ran ahead into the darkness. He thought, *Let's say I find somebody. How do I know this person's going to want to help me? . . . What kind of a person would be hanging out down here, anyway?*

That thought stopped Jack in his tracks. He thought, *What if it's some weirdo? Even a murderer . . . or some* Phantom of the Opera-*type creep, completely crazy . . . limping around with a knife . . . or an ax?*

Standing still, listening to his heart pound in the silence, Jack decided he had no choice. The light from the flashlight was definitely dimmer. He did *not* want to be down here in the dark. He had to find a way out.

Taking a fresh grip on his wooden sword, Jack went forward. He kept up a strong pace, stooping every three or four minutes to test the air current and make sure he was still on course. After about ten minutes at a brisk walk he came to a junction, a crossroads.

Stranger and stranger.

As Jack stood in the center of the junction his nose picked up a familiar scent. And he knew he wasn't imagining. It wasn't the smell of watermelon gum. Now there was the faint but unmistakable scent of peanut butter.

But the junction posed a problem. He could either walk straight or go down one of three other tunnels—one to his right, or two to his left. He tried to imagine where he was. Had he walked as far as the library—about four blocks? Or was he farther along, say, at the town hall or the small shopping area? It was impossible to know. And did he really want to try pounding on a door that might be in the basement of the town hall? Or the police station?

Jack decided to go with his nose again, but when he sniffed at the opening of each tunnel, the peanut scent seemed to be everywhere.

So starting with the tunnel on his left, and then each tunnel in order, he did the fifty-paces-stoop-and-sniff test. After about fifteen minutes of walking back and forth Jack reached a verdict. The only tunnel that had any scent at all was the one he would have taken just by going straight when he first came to the junction.

Jack sat down to rest for a few minutes. He was winded, sweating. But sitting was no good. For one thing, he started to get cold quickly, and for another, it was too quiet, too much like a tomb. Jack didn't like the thoughts that crowded into that silence. And Jack didn't like sitting on the same floor the rats scurried around on. So he got up and continued moving.

After another ten minutes Jack didn't need to stoop to smell the peanut butter. It wasn't a strong smell, but compared to how faint it had been, it seemed to Jack like he was eating a sandwich. He kept walking, careful not to let his wooden sword tap on the floor of the tunnel. After another hundred steps Jack stopped to listen. Was that a distant car horn? Was he under a street? He heard nothing but the occasional scurry of little feet. He decided to keep still for another few minutes, and he turned off his flashlight to save the batteries.

The darkness of underground places is different. Underground darkness is complete. No streetlights, no stars, no moon, no light reflected from clouds. Jack knew this. He had seen pictures of animals living in caves. Some of them gradually evolved to have no eyes at all.

With zero light the pupil of the human eye opens up so wide that the colored iris almost disappears. The eye strains to see, and without the essential ingredient—light—it sees absolutely nothing.

Jack shut his eyes, leaning against the wall opposite the big pipe. He wanted his eyes to forget the brightness of the flashlight. He wanted to experience that utter darkness, that cave darkness.

When he opened his eyes, Jack had to blink to be sure they were really open. He held up his hand, touched his nose, and then waved his hand around, just inches from his face. Nothing. He opened his eyes until he imagined they must be as big as oranges. Nothing.

Pushing away from the wall, standing in the center of the tunnel, Jack put his arms out and turned in a slow circle, eyes open wide. And an odd thing happened. As he turned it was as if there was a small, dark rectangle hanging in midair—dark, but not so dark as everything else—

and it seemed to sweep past as he turned.

Jack rotated until the dark rectangle was directly in front of his eyes, and when he stood still, so did the rectangle.

It could be only one thing. It was light. The small rectangle was the shape of the tunnel, farther on in the direction he had been walking. Somewhere up ahead there was light. And peanut butter. And what else?

Jack turned on his flashlight and walked ahead quickly—and quietly.

Chapter 19

# WALK into the Light

As Jack walked silently forward, every hundred steps or so he turned off his flashlight. The light ahead of him grew brighter.

Abruptly, he came to a T in the tunnel. And at that moment he learned why it was called the steam tunnel.

Heat radiated from the large iron pipe, and there was a faint hissing sound. Where the pipe he had been walking beside met the pipe in the new tunnel, there was a valve with a large, round handle. A steady drip of hot water had made a puddle on the floor at the junction.

There was no guesswork now. The light was coming from the left. There was enough of a glow bouncing from the walls of the tunnel that Jack turned off his flashlight to let his eyes adjust to the dimness.

The light grew stronger with every twenty paces, and coming around a 45-degree bend to the left, Jack stopped in his tracks.

It was a place where two tunnels crossed, and the junction was like a tic-tac-toe frame—four corridors meeting at a center square. In the corridor to Jack's right an old refrigerator stood against the wall below the steam pipe. Some coat hooks had been fastened to the wall beside the refrigerator, and a navy blue wool coat, a gray scarf, and a green backpack were hung up.

On the left wall of the corridor straight ahead Jack saw a folding army cot with an olive green blanket folded neatly at one end, a pillow on top of the blanket. On the tunnel wall opposite the cot there was a low wooden bookcase. A large black-and-white cat sat on the bookcase and looked at Jack with wide green eyes, a statue with a twitching tail.

In the center square a card table and one folding metal chair sat on a piece of dark green carpet. On the table lay a pencil and a newspaper turned to a half-finished crossword puzzle. There was a paper plate and a plastic knife—and an open jar of crunchy peanut butter.

In the corridor to Jack's left a tall floor lamp with a fringed shade stood beside a worn-out easy chair. The lamp was on, and in the chair sat a young man wearing black jeans and a tie-dyed T-shirt. A book lay open on his lap. Pushing a strand of long blond hair out of his eyes, he looked up as if seeing Jack appear was the most natural thing in the world. He looked curiously at Jack's sword.

"Nice sword. I've been listening to you coming for about half an hour now. Sound travels a long way down here. Was that you did all the yelling?"

Jack nodded. "Locked myself in . . . I got scared." Pointing at the peanut butter, Jack said, "Then I followed my nose." Taking a closer look, Jack guessed the boy was seventeen or eighteen. "Do you *live* here?"

The boy shook his head. "Nah, I'm just hanging out for a while."

Jack looked around. "Where did all this stuff come from? Did you bring it here?"

"Nope. I guess it's been here a long time. There's a guest list on the wall by the fridge, and it goes way back. Pretty strange."

Jack was still trying to take it all in. "But . . . I mean, like the refrigerator, and the electricity, and . . . everything. It's like a little apartment."

The kid grinned, and said with friendly sarcasm, "That's what it is. It is, in fact, like a little apartment. I think you have now understood. You have now said about all that can be said about it."

Jack didn't pick up on the sarcasm. "And . . . what about the rats?"

The kid jerked his head toward the cat. "That's Caesar's job. He comes with the place."

"So, like . . . you're *allowed* to be here?" Jack asked.

The boy shrugged. "Allowed? I don't know. And I don't care. All I know is that until my dad calms down or gets some serious help, I'm spending my nights right here. I mean, it's a little spooky, and I don't have my stereo, but it's a whole lot safer than my house is right now. And John said I could use the place, so, yeah—I guess I'm allowed."

Jack knew. Right away he knew.

But he asked to make sure. "*John* said you could use the place? John who?"

"John the janitor. Works at the old high school. He knows my dad, and last year he said if I ever needed help I should tell him. So about a week ago I needed help, and I told him, and here I am."

"You talked to John last year?"

The kid nodded. "Some of my friends said he was a good guy, so I checked him out, you know, just started shootin' the breeze with him one afternoon when I was in detention. He was working on something in the room, light switch or something. He was just easy to talk to. Like, first I just asked what he was doing, and he didn't brush me off. Really told me stuff, showed me how the circuits worked, the whole deal. I'm interested in stuff like that, and he could tell, so he just kept showing. Then he asks me my name, and I say, 'I'm Eddie Wahlson.' And that's when he tells me if I ever need help, look him up. Turns out he knows my dad from the VFW."

Jack shook his head, not understanding. "The VFW?"

Eddie said, "That little white house near the diner downtown? Has the sign? Veterans of Foreign Wars?—VFW. It's like a club for guys that were in the service, fought in wars and stuff. Guys can help each other, talk about problems and stuff. War messes a lot of guys up. Messed up my dad. He was in the National Guard, and his unit got called up for Desert Storm—the Gulf War?"

Jack nodded.

"Anyway, that's how come John knew my dad, and that's how come I'm here." Eddie was done being sociable. Standing up, he said, "You want to get out of here, right?"

Jack nodded. "Yeah. Where are we, anyway?"

Eddie said, "About a block away from the fire station. How'd you get into the tunnels? Find an open door?"

Jack said, "Sort of. At my school."

"That where you found the sword?"

Jack nodded.

Eddie nodded back and said, "Cool."

Jack pointed at the wall near the corner by the refrigerator. He took two steps closer and bent down to read. "Did you sign the guest list?"

"You bet," said Eddie. "I'm part of Huntington history now."

Jack scanned the list. He turned on his flashlight so he could read the names. They had been written on a smooth patch of white concrete with pencils and markers, even a crayon or two. Dozens of names, going all the way back to the 1970s. Then Jack did a double take: The first name on the wall was LOU CARSWELL, 1973.

Jack wanted to look at every name. But Eddie had run out of patience. "The best place to get out is where I do. John knows this guy at the fire station, and he gave me a key to the door that comes out in the basement hallway there. That's where the steam comes from—there's a big boiler at the fire station. Still heats the library and the town hall. Keeps me toasty too. So let's go."

Jack almost had to trot to keep up with Eddie's longer strides. There were no lights once they left the living area, but Eddie didn't slow down and he didn't use a flashlight. Jack thought, *Maybe Eddie is evolving. Maybe one day Eddie will have no eyes at all.*

In five minutes they came to an opening in the wall, and Eddie said, "This is it." He ducked into the opening and flipped a switch by the door. A dim bulb lit the short corridor.

Eddie listened by the door. There were voices on the other side. They got louder and then began to get fainter. Eddie pulled out a key and put it into the lock, but held up his hand. He whispered, "Wait a minute or so. Anybody sees you out there, just tell 'em you came in the back door to use the bathroom. It's right down the hall to the left."

After half a minute of silence Eddie asked, "What grade you in?"

Jack said, "Fifth."

"So you're at the old high school this year, right?"

Jack nodded.

"When you see John, tell him Eddie says hi, okay?"

Jack said, "I'll tell him."

"And listen, John's a good guy to know, like if you ever get in trouble—I mean, like, real trouble. You ought to get to know him."

Jack said, "Yeah. I'm gonna do that."

It was quiet in the hallway, so Eddie opened the door a crack.

Jack said, "Eddie, I think you should keep this

sword, okay? I don't think I better try to carry it through downtown."

Eddie took the sword and hefted it appreciatively. He nodded. "Cool."

Jack said, "Hey . . . do you have any gum, Eddie?"

Eddie reached into his pocket. "Yeah."

"What flavor?" asked Jack.

Eddie pulled out an opened pack. "Watermelon—want a piece?"

Jack smiled and said, "No, thanks."

Eddie opened the door and said, "See you, little buddy."

Jack stepped out. "So long, Eddie—thanks."

And Eddie closed the door.

Chapter 20

# TWO PLUS TWO

Outside the steam tunnel door Jack blinked in the bright bluish light. The corridor in the basement of the firehouse was empty, so he headed for the Exit sign and the stairs to his right.

Thirty seconds later Jack was standing in steadily falling snow at the corner of Maple and Williams. And then it hit him. Jack realized he must be late. He'd said he would be back at the shop at five. Looking in the window of a convenience store, Jack saw the time. It was five forty-five.

Instinctively he started running north on Williams toward Main Street. A quick fall on the snowy sidewalk and Jack realized running was not a good idea. Unhurt, he dusted himself off and then walked as quickly as he could.

Jack knew his dad would be worried. He might have even left. The school might be locked. Should he go into a store and try to call the school, or call home? He hoped his dad wouldn't be too angry, or even worse, disappointed in him again. Jack tried to pick up his pace as he continued slipping along toward the high school.

When he got to Main Street and turned east, he had to walk against the wind. It wasn't really cold, not by Minnesota standards, but the wind cut through his sweatshirt. By bending his head down, the brim of his Vikings cap kept the snow out of his face, and he only had to look up to check for cross traffic when he reached a curb.

When Jack passed the library, he picked up his pace. The sidewalk in the heart of downtown had already been sanded, so there was less danger of falling. He only had about four blocks to go.

Lifting his head to look out from under the brim of his cap, Jack saw something through the snow. At the next street, Randall Street.

A car with its lights on was parked behind the stop sign.

But it wasn't a car. It was a pickup. A green pickup.

John Rankin flashed his headlights, and Jack waved at him. Jack wanted to slow down. Thirty more steps and he would be there. *Think fast, think, think!* What could he say? No coat, no backpack, walking alone downtown in the snow.

Jack thought, *I can say I left my stuff at the*

*library, got involved in a book, saw the time, ran out-side.* Jack felt the lie strangling him, and deep down he knew it wouldn't work, knew he didn't want to try to make it work.

Jack could see the truck's wipers ticking back and forth. Jack stood at the crosswalk, waited for a salt truck to rumble past, and then crossed the street.

John Rankin rolled his window down halfway.

Jack smiled as best he could. "Hi, Dad. I—"

His dad cut him off, a sharp edge to his voice. "Come get in out of the snow, Jack."

Jack said, "But my coat and my backpack are—"

"Just get in the truck, Jack. I've got 'em."

Jack didn't understand. "My coat? . . . And my backpack?"

"Just get in." It was that angry-and-relieved voice, the kind parents only use when they've finally located a missing child.

Jack walked around the back of the truck and got in on the passenger side. As he shut the door his dad reached over and flicked the fan switch to high. In the light from one of the old downtown lampposts Jack saw his coat and backpack on the seat. He said, "You . . . you found them."

His dad said, "Yup—no thanks to you. You had me and everybody else worried sick."

John Rankin paused, getting control of himself. "I've been waiting here for about twenty minutes. About five fifteen I called home just to be sure you didn't snag a ride with a friend. Lois said you weren't there, so I started putting two and two together."

Very meekly Jack said, "Two and two?"

His dad nodded. "I checked the supply closet and saw you'd put your stuff away. Then I smelled something funny. Over behind the door. That's quite a load of gum in that pail."

Jack said, "But how—"

His dad held up his hand and said, "If you'll just hold your horses, I'll tell you. I found you because I look up from your bucket full of gum in the closet there and I see the lock on the key safe isn't latched. That's when it clicked."

John Rankin paused a few seconds, then said, "How'd you like that view from the bell tower?"

Jack gulped.

His dad went on. "That was you up there, right? On Tuesday? I thought I heard something. A school gets real quiet once the kids leave." Another pause. "So, did you like the view?"

Jack nodded. He could tell his dad wasn't really mad now, so he said, "I just wanted to see it. I never saw the whole town before."

John Rankin allowed himself to smile a little. "What gets me is that from all those keys you pick my two favorites. I've been up that tower. . . . I don't know how many times. I go up there to sit and think sometimes." Jack remembered the chair on the third landing.

"And the other key?" asked Jack. "How did you find out I had that one?"

His dad said, "Now, that was more like a lucky guess. I mean, I could have figured it out, but I would have had to get out the master key log and start counting until I found another stack that was one key short—but that would have taken me all night. It was because the tunnel key was right there near the bottom next to the tower key. I guessed that if I were you, I'd go and take one of each. And of course, I knew you were working in the auditorium. So, two plus two equals four."

"I'm sorry I made you worry, Dad."

John Rankin cleared his throat. "Well, I could see just what happened, you leaving the key in the door, and all. I went down in the tunnel with a light and I saw your footprints. I almost started yelling, and you probably could have heard me too. But I knew you wouldn't come to any harm. If I needed to find you, I knew I could. And sometimes you just have to step back and let things play out."

His dad fell silent and flipped the heater switch back to low. As the fan got quieter the rhythmic sound of the windshield wipers seemed louder.

Jack felt funny, like he was different. He wanted to tell his dad everything, and he wanted to know more. Jack said, "I met Eddie, Dad—Eddie Wahlson. I saw the place in the tunnel. And Eddie let me out the door at the fire station."

John Rankin leaned forward and released the parking brake. He pushed in the clutch, dropped the shift lever into first, and eased out onto Main Street.

And all he said was, "We'd better head home now."

## Chapter 21

# Something Permanent

It was slow-going on Main Street. The road crews were out, but the temperature was dropping quickly and the snow was coming faster than the salt could melt it.

The pickup crawled along past the library, and Jack stared out at the snow. It came rushing at the windshield. Jack loved looking up at streetlights during a snowstorm. Those millions of swirling flakes had always reminded him of a wild, happy dance.

But not now. Now they looked frantic, confused. The flakes crashed and tumbled in the air, fierce and chaotic.

Had he said something wrong? His dad was three feet away, but he seemed like he was in a distant room. Jack felt like a door had slammed in his face.

"Dad, I didn't mean to . . . I mean, about the tunnel . . . I won't tell anybody."

John Rankin looked across at him and smiled. Jack had never seen a smile like that before. His dad said, "Jackie, I know that. I know you wouldn't tell anyone. It's just that that place is . . . well, it's a whole other story. . . . And I think it's a story you're old enough to know about. . . . And when I try to think about how to tell it to you, it brings back a lot of memories." His dad looked close to tears.

Jack said, "I saw Lou's name on the wall. It said 'Lou Carswell, 1973.' Did Lou really stay there?"

John Rankin laughed and looked out his side window for a moment. "You sure do get right to the heart of things, Jackie. Yes, Lou did spend some time living down there, and that's a pretty good place to start the story. . . . But really I have to go back a few years before."

Jack knew what that meant. A few years before 1973 was when his dad had been in the army.

John Rankin said, "That time I spent in the army—that was a hard time for me. I mean, going into the service is never an easy thing, and thank God there are men and women who still take on that job. I had two tours of duty, with the infantry, down on the ground. I went through some awful times, and I lived through things I pray you or nobody else ever has to live through."

In the moving light and shadows Jack could see

his dad's jaw clenched tight. Then he took a deep breath and let it out slowly. "When I got back to Huntington after Vietnam, I was in a bad way. I was scared a lot of the time. I got sick real easy. I lived at home for a while, but my dad didn't know how to help and Mom wasn't well enough herself. I was the last thing she needed right then.

"I wasn't doing well at all, and for about a year I went and stayed at the veterans hospital this side of Minneapolis. I was just barely holding on.

"Then once, when I came down for the day to see Mom and Dad, I got it in my head to go say hello to my senior English teacher at the high school. I went to her room after school, and she wasn't there. Janitor said she'd moved to St. Paul. Well, he and I got to talking, and turns out he'd been in the same field division as me, but during the Korean War. And right out of the blue he asks me if I can work nights cleaning up at the high school. Said he really needed the help. I didn't learn till about three years later that he gave up his overtime hours to let me get back to feeling useful.

"Those nights at the school were good for me. I was in a familiar place, a place full of good memories. It was just what I needed. Tom Baldridge. That's his name. He retired about twelve years ago. I'm not just talking when I tell you that the day Tom put a broom in my hands, he saved my life."

Jack said, "Is that Lou in the picture on your dresser? And that big knife in your top drawer? Was that your knife in the army?"

John Rankin laughed out loud. "You ought to go into detective work, get paid for all your snooping. That sure is my knife, and you keep clear of it, Mister Nosyman. And yes, that's Lou in the picture. I met Lou on my second tour, and we teamed up, looked out for each other. You do a dozen or so patrols with the same person and you get to be close, like family. I carried a letter to his parents and his girlfriend, and he carried a letter to my folks, just in case. We used to joke that we kept each other alive because we neither of us wanted to have to deliver those letters. But when I got out at the end of my hitch, Lou still had another twelve months to go.

"Lou was from Chicago, and after he'd been home awhile, he came up to visit me. He needed work, and he needed a place to stay where he wouldn't be a bother to anyone. So that's when I rigged up that place in the tunnel. Friend of mine at the fire station helped me and Lou get the place fitted out, and I helped Lou get a job working nights cleaning up at the town hall. Once he had steady work, he moved into a rented room, but we left all the stuff in the tunnel. A few years later there was an opening at the high school. So that's the story of Lou Carswell."

They were only about three blocks from Greenwood Street, and Jack still had so many questions. "What about all the other names?" he asked. "It's a long list. Are all the others your friends too?"

His dad nodded. "My friends, Lou's friends, sometimes it's a kid like Eddie, caught in a hard spot, needs a safe place for a few days. A lot of people know that place is there, and when there's a need, someone gets in touch."

"A lot of people know?" asked Jack. "What if someone told the principal or the school committee—or the police? Don't you think it's probably against the law?"

John Rankin smiled. It felt odd to have his son worried about him for a change. "Well, I've looked into that, and as far as I can tell, the only thing I might be guilty of is using some town electricity. I put in an electric meter right at the get-go, and every month since October of 1973 I've been paying the going rate in a cash donation to the annual Veterans Day parade fund, and I keep careful records. Anyone wants to take me to court, I'm all set. I think I can pull together a pretty good group of witnesses." Then with a wink he said, "Now, you on the other hand—*you* just might have to go to jail for having a pocket full of keys. But don't you think we could get Mr. Ackerby to testify that you're a genuine temporary janitor?"

"And a darn good one, too," said Jack with a grin, "just like you."

Jack and his dad were still laughing as the truck turned into the snowy driveway at 920 Greenwood Street. Above the basketball backboard on the garage the floodlights were lit. As the pickup came to a stop Jack looked through the windshield, up into the light, and he saw millions of flakes swirling in a wild, happy dance.

Helen Rankin pulled aside the curtain above the sink and looked out the back window. She saw two boys get out of the truck. Or was it two men?

As they came toward the house John Rankin carried Jack's backpack in one hand, and his other hand was on his son's shoulder to steady himself.

They were trying to catch snowflakes on their tongues, laughing, almost falling down.

Helen was struck with the image. Her first baby, her little Jack, didn't seem so little. Somehow he was older, stronger.

And her husband, her best friend, her own

John—he seemed younger, less burdened.

Helen knew what she was looking at.

This wasn't an illusion. It wasn't a fleeting sensation. It wasn't something exclusive happening across the border in Boy Territory.

Helen was completely familiar with what she was seeing.

It was something good, something permanent.

It was love.

With a full heart Helen let the curtain fall back into place.

Walking to the front of the house, she called up the stairs, "Lois—they're home. Come for dinner now."

Then she went back to the kitchen to open the door for Jack and his dad.

Here's a preview of
ANDREW CLEMENTS'S

# *THE* SCHOOL STORY

# Fan Number One

Natalie couldn't take it. She peeked in the door-way of the school library, then turned, took six steps down the hall, turned, paced back, and stopped to look in at Zoe again. The suspense was torture.

Zoe was still reading. The first two chapters only added up to twelve pages. Natalie leaned against the door frame and chewed on her thumbnail. She thought, *What's taking her so long?*

Zoe could see Natalie out of the corner of her eye. She could feel all that nervous energy nudging at her, but Zoe wasn't about to be rushed. She always read slowly, and she liked it that way, especially when it was a good story. And this one was good.

### The Cheater by Natalie Nelson
### page 12

I catch up with Sean between Eighty-second and Eighty-first Streets. His legs are longer than mine, so I'm panting. I grab his arm and he stops in front of a bodega.

He says, "Why are you following me?"

"I've got to talk to you."

"Yeah, well, too bad. You had your chance to talk during the Penalty Board hearing. And you didn't."

"But if I told the truth, then the whole school would know I cheated. I'd get expelled."

He just looks at me. "But you really did cheat, right? . . . And I really didn't steal that answer key, right? . . . And you know I didn't steal it because *you* did, right?"

I nod yes to all the questions.

Sean is almost shouting now, his eyes wild. "So first you steal, then you cheat, and now you've lied. And me? You've left me to take the punishment."

The shopkeeper is worried. He moves from the counter to the doorway of the bodega, looking at us.

Sean ignores him and gets right into my face, screaming. "Well, guess what, Angela. We're not friends now—and I don't know if we ever were!"

He storms away, hands jammed in his pockets, shoulders hunched, stabbing the sidewalk with every step.

Me, I cry.


Zoe let page twelve slip onto the table and then stared at it, deep in thought.

"So, what do you think?"

Natalie was right behind her, and Zoe jumped six inches. "Jeez, Natalie! Scare me to death! And you ruined a nice moment too."

"But what do you think? Is it any good?"

Zoe nodded. "I think it's very good."

"Really?" Natalie pulled out a chair and sat down, leaning forward. "I mean, you're not just saying that because we're best friends?"

Zoe shook her head. "No, I mean it. It's good. Like I can't wait to read the whole thing. Can you bring the rest tomorrow?"

Natalie smiled and reached into her back-pack. She pulled out a blue folder with a rubber band around it. "Here. I've still got to write about five more chapters. I just needed to know if the beginning was any good, but you can read what I've got done if you want."

Zoe took the folder carefully and said, "This is great. But you *are* going to finish it, right? Do you know the whole story already—like all the way to the end?"

Natalie said, "Not *all* the way to the end . . . but almost. I know how the end *feels*, but not exactly what happens—at least, not yet."

Natalie's book had begun by accident on the bus with her mom late one afternoon back in

September. Sixth grade was already three weeks old, and both she and her mom had settled into the routine of commuting together. It was a Friday afternoon, and they were going home on the 5:55 coach, thundering through the Lincoln Tunnel from New York City to Hoboken, New Jersey.

Her mom looked exhausted. Natalie studied the face tilted toward her on the headrest. It was a pretty face—*Prettier than mine*, she thought. But there were little lines at the corners of her mother's eyes and mouth. Care lines, worry lines.

Natalie said, "Hard day, Mom?"

Eyes still closed, her mom smiled and nodded. "The editorial department met all day with the marketing department—all day."

Natalie asked, "How come?" When her dad died, Natalie had decided she needed to talk to her mom more. Sometimes she pretended to be interested in her mom's work at the publishing company even when she wasn't. Like now.

Her mom said, "Well, the marketing people keep track of what kinds of books kids and parents and teachers are buying. Then they tell us, and we're supposed to make more books like the ones they think people will buy."

Natalie said, "Makes sense. So, what kinds of books do they want you to make?"

Hannah Nelson lifted her head off the seat back and turned toward Natalie. "Here's the summary of a six-hour meeting. Ready?"

Natalie nodded.

Her mom used a deep voice that sounded bossy. "People, we need to publish more adventure books, more series books, and more school stories." In her regular voice she said, "That was it. A six-hour meeting for something that could have gone into a one-page memo—or a three-line E-mail."

Then Natalie asked, "What's a school story?"

"A school story is just what it sounds like—it's a short novel about kids and stuff that happens mostly at school."

Natalie thought for a second and then said, "You mean like *Dear Mr. Henshaw*?"

And her mom said, "Exactly."

Then Natalie said to herself, *Hey, who knows more about school than someone who's right there, five days a week, nine months a year? I bet I could write a school story.*

And that was all it took. Natalie Nelson the novelist was born.

Or almost born. Her career as an author didn't officially spring to life until about four months later—on that afternoon in the school library after Zoe read the first two chapters.

Because it's the same for every new author, for every new book. Somebody has to be the first to read it. Somebody has to be the first to say she likes it. Somebody has to be that first fan.

And of course, that was Zoe.

# CHAPTER 2

# A Portrait of the Author as a Young Girl

**Deary School**

IDENTIFICATION

## Nelson
## Natalie

GRADE SIX

Some people are writers, and some people are talkers. Natalie had always been a writer.

Like all writers, first she was a reader. As a baby and then a toddler, Natalie loved it when her mom or dad read to her. She loved how the same story would change, depending on who was reading it.

Mom read calmly, evenly, thoughtfully. Even if the story was exciting or scary or sad, Natalie always felt warm and safe when Mom was reading.

But not with Dad. He was loud and reckless. He made funny voices for all the firemen and ducks and princesses. He made sound effects for the trains and the caterpillars, and if the words weren't exciting or silly or scary enough, he threw in some new ones. When Dad was reading, anything could happen.

And so Natalie got her first taste of reading in the very best way, from people who loved good books almost as much as they loved her.

By the time she was four, Natalie couldn't wait any longer. She wanted more stories than her parents had time to read to her. She already knew her ABCs, and she made her mom and dad point at every word as they read to her. Then Natalie would sit and turn the pages of her picture books again and again. She started being able to see the words and hear the sounds they made, and once she began to crack the code, there was no stopping her. Natalie became a reader.

Even after Natalie could read by herself, her mom and dad read stories to her at bedtime—Dad one night, and Mom the next. Natalie always got to choose the story from her shelf of favorites.

The car crash changed all that. Natalie was in second grade, and after the accident there was only Mom to read at bedtime. And that was when Natalie hid some of her favorite books in the back of her closet. She didn't want her mom to read them anymore. Those were Daddy's books. Sometimes late at night, or on a quiet Sunday afternoon, Natalie would open up *The Sailor Dog* or *The Grouchy Ladybug*, and she could hear her father's voice reading to her.

The writing part came gradually, naturally. At first it was imitation. If Natalie read a good poem, she tried to make up one like it. If a character grabbed her imagination, Natalie would talk to her stuffed animals and pretend she was the Sailor Dog or the Steadfast Tin Soldier or Raggedy Ann. She would act out parts of a story and make up words for everyone to say. Sometimes she pretended to be Gretel, helping Hansel push the wicked witch into the oven. Other times she pretended to be the wicked witch.

And always, always, Natalie thought about the authors. She thought about Hans Christian Andersen or Margaret Wise Brown or Beatrix Potter, and she imagined these people sitting in a garden or a cabin or an attic, making up new stories. And she knew that one day she would sit down in a garden or a cabin or an attic and try it out for herself.

When Natalie got to fourth grade, she began to spend more time writing. She made herself a little writing place in the back corner of the loft that she and her mom had moved to. Her desk was a door laid flat across two small filing cabinets. She sat in her dad's old red desk chair and used his old Macintosh computer. Not quite a cabin or an attic, but close enough—and it was as close as Natalie could get to her dad.